Wenonah's Stories for Children

Clara Louise Burnham &
Warren Proctor

Copyright © 2023 Culturea Editions
Text and cover : © public domain
Edition : Culturea (Hérault, 34)
Contact : infos@culturea.fr
Print in Germany by Books on Demand
Design and layout : Derek Murphy
Layout : Reedsy (https://reedsy.com/)
ISBN : 9791041829309
Légal deposit : July 2023

CHAPTER I.

LOIS AND HAROLD.

When Lois and Harold Robbins first learned that they were not going to the seashore this summer they felt very much disappointed.

Lois was ten years old and Hal was eight. They thought there was no fun so nice as wading in the salt water and letting the foam break over their legs. Of course it was better still to have Daddy put the water-wings on them and let them float, and give them swimming lessons. They had not quite learned to swim alone yet without the water-wings, and this was to be the summer when they would surely do it.

When their father saw their disappointment he tried to cheer them up.

"Don't you know that Lake Michigan looks as big as the ocean?" he asked.

"It isn't salt," said Lois.

"Has it any starfish and crabs in it?" asked Hal.

"No," returned Mr. Robbins, "but children can swim in it and wade on the sandy shore, and then there are sweet-smelling pine woods to play in, and your mother wants to smell those pines. Don't you think you would like to see a little more of the world, instead of going to the same place every summer?"

Lois shook her head very decidedly. "No," she replied, "for I know we shall never have such a good time as we do at the seashore."

Her father smiled. "It is never a wise plan to make up your mind not to have a good time," he said. "That is like turning a bowl upside down. Nothing can run into it, so it stays empty. Keep your bowls right side up, both of you, and you can't tell what jolly things may run into them. Hal, you remember those pictures of Indians we were looking at last night?"

Hal at once became interested. He always wanted to hear all he could about Indians.

"Well, don't you think it will be pleasant to see that country where the Indians roamed, and led their wild, free life long after they were gone from New England?"

"What do you mean by holding our bowls right side up?" asked the little boy.

"If you are hopeful and cheerful and loving every morning and all day," replied his father, "you are holding your bowl right side up."

"Do you think if I do that in Michigan an Indian might fall into it?"

His father laughed. "I think the Indians have cleared out from there; but you will see the trails they used through the woods, the places where their tents stood, the water where their canoes moved so silently, the shores where their moccasins trod so swiftly, and breathe the clear, fine air through which their wild whoops rang as they danced around the camp fire, while the smoke curled up above the tall trees."

"I say we go, Lois," said Hal, his eyes shining.

"If the Indians were there now," said his sister, "I think you would run in the other direction."

"No, I wouldn't," returned Hal confidently. "I'd put on one of those great big war bonnets and tell them I wanted to be a brave and live with them, and I think they'd let me; but I don't think they'd take you, Lois, for they like braves a great deal better than they do squaws."

"I wouldn't be a squaw," returned Lois. "I would be an Indian princess and wear a wonderful red mantle with purple stripes and have chains about my neck, and my hair braided and shining, and beautiful bracelets, and they would all bow down to me—and you'd have to, too."

"No, the chief would take me for his son and I should have a wonderful bow, the longest in the tribe, and shoot my arrows so straight that the other Indians would all say 'Ugh! ugh!' That's what they say when they like anything, isn't it, Daddy?"

"I think it is," returned Mr. Robbins, and Harold ran to get the Indian book to show his sister how he would look shooting arrows before an admiring tribe, because he had found that picture last night, and it had pleased him very much indeed. He found the picture of a princess for Lois and she liked the looks of the straight-nosed beauty, because her own nose turned up a little, and she thought it would be fine to have such a handsome nose and hold her head so proudly. It was almost impossible to hold one's head proudly if one had a turn-up nose.

Her father patted her shoulder as he passed her to leave the room.

"That's right," he said. "Have a good time being a princess this summer, instead of a mermaid. I'll get you a tent if you want it."

CHAPTER II.

WENONAH.

When they took the train to go West to Michigan, Lois and Hal were very much interested in the sleeping car. They had never seen one before, and when their father tucked them into two opposite upper berths that night, they hardly wanted to go to sleep, it was such fun to peek out at each other between the heavy curtains.

The children's heads were still full of the subject of the Indians. They felt they were on their way to the home of the red man, and Lois said to her father:

"What would the Indians have thought of these little upstairs beds?"

Hal was leaning out into the aisle from his couch. "They'd have said 'Wow! wow!'" he cried.

"Softly," suggested his father. "Not only the Indians would have been surprised. Think of the first white people going slowly and patiently across the country in their covered wagons, taking weeks to travel over the distance we cover in a day. Isn't it wonderful to live now instead of then?"

"But that was the most fun," said Hal. "I've seen pictures of the Indians galloping across the plain to attack the wagons, but the men had their guns and they saved themselves and drove the Indians off."

Mrs. Robbins had the berth underneath Harold and she looked out between her curtains.

"You know the sooner you go to sleep, children, the sooner you will see Lake Michigan," she said.

They had always found that their mother knew what she was talking about, and they were eager to see the Indians' lake, so they turned over in their little up-stairs beds and in a surprisingly short few minutes it was morning.

The next night they spent in another sort of little beds, only this time they were on a large steamer on a lake that stretched away as far as they could see, just like the ocean. The children could scarcely believe that those great waves were not salt.

"What would an Indian in his little canoe have thought to see a big mountain of a ship like this coming along toward him?" asked Hal.

His father shook his head. "The canoes kept near the shore, I suspect. You will see the sort of shore tomorrow."

When they arrived at their destination the children were pleased to find a sandy beach, and the foaming surf which looked good to wade in.

They found a little log cabin waiting for them and it was nestled in pine woods on the side of a hill. Their father was busy at the wharf some time about the luggage, and when he arrived at the house he looked at the children with a laugh in his eyes but his lips very sober.

"What do you think I have just found out?" he asked when the men had brought the trunks and gone away.

The children listened eagerly. They liked this forest hill full of Christmas trees, with enough spaces in front of the cabin to look through to the blue lake, and they could hardly wait to hear what their father had to tell them.

"What is it? What is it?" they asked together.

"Have you been holding your bowls right side up all the morning? Have they, Mother?" he asked, turning to his wife, who was examining the way the little windows opened like doors.

"Yes, they have been very good children," she returned, with her attention on the hinges and fastenings.

"Very well, then. I must tell you that there is an Indian camp here."

The eyes of both Lois and Harold became very large. Their father looked serious.

"Are we going to stay?" asked Hal in a hushed voice.

"Is it safe?" asked Lois in the same breath.

"I think we can risk it," said Mr. Robbins.

Hal shook his head. "We'd better each have a gun then," he said, "because we must sleep some of the time."

His father laughed and gave both the children a hug. "You keep your bowls right side up and you won't need any guns," he said. "The Indians are like other people in that. They will give you the same sort of treatment you give them."

"See here, dear, will you?" said Mrs. Robbins to her husband. "What is the matter with this catch?"

"They had better make the windows safe," said Hal to Lois in a low tone. His eyes were still very large. "Come out and see if we can see any smoke."

The children went outside and peered about among the trees.

"I think Daddy seems very queer and careless about this, don't you?" asked Lois. "They must be tame Indians."

"They may pretend to be," said Hal, "but I don't see how he can trust them in the night time."

"See here, children," called their mother from the door, "don't stray away until I get your play clothes out of the trunk."

Lois and Hal went inside and quite silently changed their traveling clothes for tougher garments, then they again went out doors.

Their parents had bought the children wrist watches in leather straps before coming here, because they knew it was a wild country and it was so hard for them to remember the time of day. The father and mother were very busy now unpacking and settling the little home, so they merely reminded Lois and Hal to remember to be at home by six o'clock.

"Did you notice how near the hotel is?" asked Mr. Robbins, "Come out here." He showed them what they had not observed: a glimpse between the thick trees of a large spreading building, built of logs just like their own little house.

"So if you get lost just ask somebody to direct you to the hotel. Understand?"

The children nodded and he went back to his work of hanging a hammock among the trees. Mrs. Robbins had come West in need of rest, and her husband intended her to live in this hammock, as much as possible.

"I think Daddy acts very queer," said Lois as the two moved slowly away on the narrow forest path.

"This looks to me like an Indian trail," said Hal quite gloomily.

"That is what it is, of course," replied Lois. "The idea of Daddy saying so coolly if we get lost to ask for the hotel—and these woods full of Indians!"

"And we begged to go to the seashore, too," responded Hal.

They held each other by the hand and moved slowly. The piney air about them was delicious, and every few steps they would get another glimpse of the light blue of the dancing waves.

"I thought you wanted to see the Indians so much, Hal, and be a 'brave,'" said Lois at last.

He hesitated a little, but he knew that being a boy he ought to protect his sister, and he felt that she was being disappointed in him.

"Of course," he began, "if I had a war-bonnet and a bow and arrows—but all I have to slap 'em with is a wrist watch."

Lois started to laugh at this, but her laugh was quickly hushed and she and Hal stopped suddenly and clung more tightly together, for among the trees a dash of scarlet was visible. It was moving swiftly and came toward them.

They suddenly saw an Indian maiden on whom they gazed with all their eyes. She wore the vivid scarlet mantle with purple stripes that Lois had longed for, and a petticoat embroidered with bright beads. Her long, shining braids hung over her shoulders. Her arms bore heavy bracelets and her silent feet were shod with moccasins. She wore a brilliant hued bodice and a narrow gold band passed across her forehead.

To the children she looked all that was stately and beautiful and commanding as she moved, straight as an arrow, through the forest. They clutched each other, with beating hearts.

She caught sight of them, and turned and they saw that she carried on her arm a large light basket, containing a few smaller ones made of sweet grass.

"You like to buy some baskets?" she asked, and wonder of wonders she smiled upon them, and drew nearer.

Lois found her voice after a minute. It had seemed to be buried somewhere deep down, perhaps in her stomach—it felt queer.

"We haven't any money," she said, hoping the announcement would not bring down the wrath of the beautiful being.

But the stranger only nodded pleasantly.

"The little boy would like some bow and arrows, perhaps?" She fixed a bright gaze on Hal, whose knees were trying not to wobble.

"Yes, I would—" he said rather breathlessly, "some day—when—when I have some money."

"You come, see what we have," said the maiden, and the children, still clasping hands, followed her stately tread.

They exchanged a look. She was doubtless luring them to the camp where the braves were perhaps at the present moment doing a war dance about a fire. If they turned back, however, and refused, she might be angry; so they followed on and determined to be so polite that no one, not even Indians, could be offended with them.

They had not gone far when the canvas of a few tents came into view. A wigwam stood in the center of the group and half a dozen Indians in native dress and shining hair that hung on their shoulders were moving about.

The Indian maiden turned and gave the children another smile, and the indifference of the other Indian faces soothed their timidity. She led them to the wigwam which proved to be a show-room for the wares they had to sell. There were baskets of every shape and size, little birch bark canoes, bows and arrows, napkin rings and many other trinkets made of birch bark or sweet grass.

"I shall tell my father and mother about these," said Lois, "I'm sure they will let us have some."

"Have you any war bonnets?" asked Hal.

"Yes, we have, but my people keep them for festival days," replied the Indian girl.

She spoke such good English and the other Indians, men and women, took so little notice of the children that they both decided in their own minds that there would not be any danger, even in the night.

Their guide, noticing the eagerness with which they gazed at her, invited them to her own tent.

"We never saw any Indians before," said Hal. "We live in Boston."

"Well, it is pleasant to travel," replied the girl, and she led them to one of the tents and took them inside. There was a bed and a wash-stand and two chairs in it, but above all there was a delicious odor which they inhaled as if they could not get enough of it.

"That is the dried sweet grass," said the maiden. "I make the baskets with that." She dropped the large light basket off her arm. "I take them to the hotel every afternoon, after the ladies take their naps," she smiled again at the children. "They feel very bright and happy then, and they buy my baskets. See how few I have brought back? Then in the mornings I work."

"O, may we see you do it sometime?"

"Certainly you may. I am going to finish one now. There is one chair for the little girl and for the boy there is the floor." She gave Hal one of her bright smiles as she said it, and he dropped down, watching the strange, dark being with admiring eyes. Among the men Indians he had not seen one who fulfilled his idea of a "Brave" but this maid was more beautiful than any Indian Princess he had imagined.

"Now let us know all of our names," said the maiden as she seated herself and pulled toward her the unfinished basket, upon which she began to weave.

"My name is Harold, but they call me Hal, because my father's name is Harold, and my mother likes to know us apart; and my sister's name is Lois. Please tell us yours."

The Indian girl smiled at her work. "My name is Wenonah. I went to a great school down in Virginia and there a teacher showed me the poem of Hiawatha. I have the name of his beautiful mother."

"I like it," said Hal promptly.

"So do I," added Lois.

"Then we all know each other now," said the girl. "Quick, that ship going by! Isn't it a picture?"

They looked through the avenue of pines that led to the beach and were just in time to see the white sails of a yacht flying like a great white bird past the opening.

"We have to taste of that water to see if it truly isn't salt," said Lois.

"Can you swim?" asked her new friend.

"We are learning to."

"Ah, that is good for the mothers." Wenonah gave Hal a mischievous nod. "Little boys sometimes do not like their bath. It is too much trouble."

Lois laughed. "How did you guess that?" she asked. "We go barefooted in summer and at night Hal always makes a fuss about washing his dusty feet."

Hal looked rather shamefacedly down at the shoes he had not yet discarded for the season.

"I knew a boy once who felt that way. Something strange happened to him."

The children pricked up their ears.

"Would you mind telling us about it?" asked Lois. If there were any stories under that gold band that went around Wenonah's forehead, they were eager to have them.

"Was he an Indian?" asked Hal.

"No, he was a white boy. I'll tell you about him."

CHAPTER III.

DUSTY FEET.

You never saw a kinder, sweeter woman than Joe's mother. His name was Joseph but of course nobody called him that. He was a jolly, happy boy with lots of freckles on his nose, and one reason he was so happy, though he never stopped to think about that, was that he had such a kind mother.

He lived on a farm, and his short trousers were held on by one suspender, as barefooted, he ran about from morning until night. Plenty of other boys came to play with him and one reason was that the kind mother nearly always had time, with all her work, to stop and spread a thick slice of bread and butter for a boy to eat.

"Dear little fellows, they're growing," she would say to herself, whenever Joe asked.

He and the other boys went fishing in the creek and played they were Indians in the woods. They climbed on the barn roof; they ran swift express trains, and when Joe had his chores to do there was usually some boy ready to help him do them.

He had to feed the pigs, squealing under the barn, and at evening go to fetch the cows. After such an active day it is no wonder that after supper every night Joe soon became drowsy.

While his mother washed the supper dishes he would get into a big calico covered arm chair, and those legs that had run about so busily all day long would feel as if they couldn't move, and his eyes would blink and stare, and close, before he knew it.

When her work was done his mother would say, "Come, Joe, come now. It is time to wash your feet and get ready for bed."

And Joe would pull his eyes open and stretch, and say, "O, Ma, why do I have to wash my feet every night?"

Day after day those nimble feet of Joe's stepped into all sorts of places all over the farm, and night after night he argued for a long time before he would wash them.

One evening when his mother had put all her clean dishes away she went over to the arm chair and Joe was so sound asleep that her gentle shaking did not wake him; so she just smiled down on him in that very nice way mothers have and decided to have pity on the child.

She threw a large apron over him and blowing out the lamp, left him to spend the night in the big, soft old chair.

Very early in the morning Joe woke up, cramped in his small quarters, and rather cold; so he crept upstairs and crawled into bed without disturbing anyone, and without washing his feet.

When morning came and the family had eaten breakfast, Joe's busy mother said nothing about last evening, and he rushed out to play without worrying his head about yesterday's dust; for this was vacation time and Joe knew that the end of it would soon come, and back to school he must go. So he and his playmates worked as hard as ever, playing ball, and climbing trees and leap frogging over each others' backs, and eating any quantity of bread and butter.

Of course that night he was again very drowsy and when his mother called him to get ready for bed, he remembered the evening before and how he had slept half the night under the old apron, and how he had not washed his feet. He became quite wide awake thinking about it, and he began to picture a heaven where boys whose legs were too heavy to move at night would never hear anyone remind them to scrub the dust off their ten toes. He began to try to think of a way to make such a heaven; and a plan came into his head.

So while his mother was finishing the dishes and calling him to go, he staggered out of his chair, and seeming to be half asleep and half awake stumbled into the front room where the sofa was, and with a groan of fatigue he fell upon its soft old springs and stretched himself out.

He thought he knew what would happen, and sure enough it really did. The kind mother, coming in later found him enjoying such a deep, peaceful sleep that she hadn't the heart to waken the boy and make him go and put his feet into cold water. She shivered a little herself, just to think of it. So she covered him up carefully with a shawl and left him.

A very strange thing happened then. Joe found that he was not lying on the sofa at all, but on a bench in a beautiful garden. Who had such a garden in their neighborhood? He knew he had never seen it before and he gazed about at the nodding lilies and the roses that climbed high on a lattice, just as they did in a picture book he had. There were paths leading about this garden and small blue flowers grew thickly along their edges.

Joe was wonderfully comfortable and happy in the midst of so much beauty, and he lay there looking at the bees seeking for honey in the flower cups, and the butterflies that played together in the air, and alighted on the flowers, sipping the dew, while they opened and closed their golden wings.

Suddenly there came into sight a lovely little girl, strolling along the path toward him. Joe was so surprised and delighted to see her that he sat right up. He remembered her well. She was the girl whom he had seen ride, standing on a milk white horse in the circus a few weeks ago. O that proud horse, with his fine arched neck, and O, the wonderful girl in the white, lacy dress, and the gold star on her forehead! How fearlessly she had smiled. To think that she should be here!

She was smiling now at the flowers as she strolled along, and butterflies circled around that golden star as it gleamed in the sunlight. Her lacy dress blew in the summer breeze, just as it had in her flight on the milk white horse.

Joe sat up and gazed and gazed. He could hardly wait to tell her how glad he was she had come, and ask her if he might ride once on her wonderful horse. He was springing up to go to meet her, when a fairy suddenly appeared from the lily-bell near him. The fairy had wings brighter than the butterflies, and a blue-bell was perched on his saucy head.

At least he seemed saucy to Joe, for he waved him back with the wand in his tiny hand, with as much an air of authority as if he had been six feet tall.

"But I want to speak to her," said Joe, "I want to play with her."

The little girl had come quite near now, and she heard this. Her smiling face grew very sober as she looked at him, and she shook her head.

"No, I must never play with boys with dusty feet," she said, and lifting the gold star on her forehead very high, she passed down another flowery path and disappeared.

The fairy smiled (he looked mischievous) and waved his wand. In a second, Joe was standing in the middle of a big puddle of sticky mud. His face grew red with shame and disappointment and he felt tears pressing hard at the back of his eyes, but of course he could not be a cry baby.

The mud seemed to get tangled with strings and they got in between his toes when he tried to pull his feet out, and then he saw that it was his mother's apron that was all smeared with mud, and turning around in distress he saw her shawl; the very one she had thrown over him on the sofa. He tried to get free of the black stickiness and step over on to the shawl when his toes trod on something that felt like an old shoe, and how he did wish for his shoes and stockings!

Suddenly he felt cold and shivered. The mud turned into snow, and his feet were so cold that he tried to wriggle his toes and found he couldn't. They were numb. He couldn't feel that he had any toes; and just then the beautiful little girl came walking slowly back, and O, how he felt, standing there, splashed with the mud he had spattered all over himself trying to get out of the puddle.

He must not cry, for that would be worse than being dirty. She might think he was in the dirt by accident, but no accident would excuse a boy for crying.

She stood there, looking at him, not scornfully as before, but with a pitying, kindly look, and all at once she began to float up from the ground.

She poised, suspended in the air, leaning over him with such sweet sadness in her gentle eyes that he became frightened and awoke with a start.

It was morning and his mother was gazing down on him with her kind smile.

He looked up sheepishly and blinked his eyes. "Mother dear," he said, and he reached up for her hand, "I guess I forgot to wash my feet."

CHAPTER IV.

BASKET MAKING.

When the children reached home they were much excited.

"We've found a gentle Indian," cried Hal.

"And she's a princess and her name is Wenonah," added Lois.

"Did she tell you she was a princess?" asked their mother.

"No, but she surely is," said Lois fervently. "She has a princess's clothes and a gold crown; and the most wonderful thing is I wished for her. I could see the sky from my bed last night and when I saw the first star I wished the way I always do:

"Starlight, Star bright,

First star I've seen tonight,

Wish you may, wish you might

Give me the wish I wish tonight."

and I wished for an Indian princess."

"Yes, she did, because she told me so coming home," said Hal earnestly.

"And to think she was waiting here and she can talk English as well as you do," said Lois. "She makes baskets and sells them at the hotel."

"And there wasn't any tomahawk in her tent, because I looked," said Hal, "and the other Indians all looked so tame, I don't believe they have any, either."

"She told us a story," said Lois. She looked at her brother and laughed, "It was about a boy who didn't like to wash his feet."

"I don't care," returned Hal, growing red, "Perhaps she can tell another story about a girl who doesn't like to make beds."

"A story already," said their father. "Well, I think those bowls of yours must have been right side up. We must go and visit her Highness and buy a basket."

"I'm going to help her carry them to the hotel," said Hal who had very much liked the Indian girl with the flashing smile, and the clothes like the bright plumage of a bird.

"I shall go, too," said Lois.

Mr. and Mrs. Robbins looked at one another and smiled. The children's earnestness and their red cheeks showed them that it would be a good plan to make a visit to the dusky maiden with whom Lois and Hal were wishing to spend so much time.

So the next day the children, escorted by their parents, went to the camp and the Indians were very much pleased to see them, because they called for Wenonah and she took them to the wigwam, where they bought a number of the pretty wares for the children and themselves.

Then they went back to Wenonah's tent with her, and watched her weave the sweet grass into the basket she was making. She told them of the school she had attended, and how she had come home and helped her people to better ways of living. She said they made a great store of their goods during the winter, then in summer went to the resorts and sold them. The weaving they did here did not amount to much, except to show the ladies and gentlemen how the baskets were made, and to give them lessons when they wished.

"How would you children like to take lessons in basket making?" asked their father.

Lois and Hal eagerly replied that they would like it very much.

"They could not manage the fine work at first," said Wenonah. "I have the coarser raffia for them."

So that is how the children came to take lessons in basket making. Their parents were not willing that they should go to the hotel to help sell the pretty things, so while Wenonah was busy there, they played on the beach or in the woods and sometimes went sailing with their father.

If Wenonah had been a white maiden they would have enjoyed being with her, for she was gentle and patient and liked fun too, but with her dark features, shining braids of hair, and silent moccasins, and the stately grace with which she moved about through the woods, they thought her the most charming person they had ever known.

Of course, sitting in the door of Wenonah's tent with the billows of the lake glinting among the trees and the fresh breeze blowing, was a very pleasant way to learn basket making; and their clumsy little hands were kindly guided by the slender, dark, clever fingers of their teacher.

Of course when the children were well started on their work it occurred to them that Wenonah might tell them another story, and Lois, feeling so well acquainted with her now, told her how she had wished on the first star that night on the steamer, and the Indian girl thought the wishing verse amusing, so

Lois taught it to her, proud to think that she could teach the princess something.

"I shall wish every night after this," said Wenonah. "I wonder if that might be the reason there is so often a star on the end of a fairy's wand."

"Is there one?" asked both the children at once.

"Yes, usually. You see, the wand gives them everything they want, and perhaps it is the star that does it. I don't know, though," said Wenonah, looking thoughtfully at the sweet grass she was weaving and which made the tent smell like a field of new-mown hay. "The wand that Peter found had no star on it."

"What Peter?" asked Hal.

"What wand?" asked Lois.

So, of course, Wenonah, being very polite and obliging, began to tell them about it.

CHAPTER V.

THE WAND.

What a pleasant thing it is to be able to say of a boy, He is the strongest boy in the village—or the most honest boy in the village—or the kindest boy in the village—or, nicest of all,—He is the best boy in the village; and what a sad thing it is to say of a boy, He is the worst boy in the village; and that is what everybody said of Peter.

He was a tease and a bully—and a bully is always a coward, you know. The little girls at school avoided him. They never knew what minute he would pull their hair, or stick out his foot suddenly and trip them up.

The animals feared him, and the meanest thing a boy can do, even worse than pulling a little girl's hair, is to be unkind to animals, or even to tease them. No boy who likes to play fair will do it; for animals cannot speak, or defend themselves.

Peter's dog wanted to love him, as dogs always do, but he couldn't trust his master. When they went out together, the dog, whose name was Pat, followed at a little distance. He wanted to go with Peter, but he was afraid of the heavy shoe that could suddenly fly out and hurt him.

So Peter lost all the best part of life by being sulky and dishonest and spending his time thinking up mischievous things to do. There was another boy in the village where Peter lived whom he especially disliked. This boy's name was Lawrence, and the reason Peter hated him was that although smaller than himself, Lawrence had once or twice jumped to the defence of some girl or boy whom Peter was hurting, and driven the bigger boy off with his fists.

Peter was scowling and thinking about Lawrence one day as he was trudging along the dusty road, Pat following at a safe distance. The dog was hoping that pretty soon his master wouldn't look so cross and that he would dare to go closer. Once in a while when Peter felt good-natured he used to throw sticks for Pat to run after and bring back, and Pat loved that.

Well, Peter trudged along with his hands in his pockets, but not whistling as happy boys do. His eyes were on the dusty road as he thought about Lawrence and wished he could beat him. He had once found a penny as he walked along this road and he was thinking about that, too, and wishing he could find another. He began to wonder what he would buy with it if he could find one.

All at once he noticed a shining little object lying by the roadside. He went toward it and Pat noticed his movement and saw as quickly as Peter did that the shining object was a little stick. The dog's ears and tail went up gladly. If Peter was going to pick up a stick, that meant that he would throw it and they would have a game. Pat ran in front of Peter and got in his way and the impatient boy gave him a kick.

Down went Pat's ears and tail, and crying out, he ran away to a safe distance, while Peter stooped to the strange, small, shining object. It was very smooth and looked like silver. It was probably more valuable than a penny, and the boy picked it up. He would hide it and wait to see if he could hear anything of the owner, and then make him pay a good price for it.

Peter's eyes shone with satisfaction at this thought, and he picked up the silver stick. It was different from anything he had ever seen and he wondered what its owner used it for.

He had no sooner grasped it and stood up than he began to sail gently up into the air. He was so astonished that his eyes nearly fell out; but it was pleasant, too, to be wafted gently up and up as if he were a fluff of thistledown instead of a clumsy country boy with the heavy shoes that poor Pat feared.

Little by little the road and trees and houses and barns and broad fields below him faded out of sight. "How far can I go?" wondered Peter, and he grasped the satin-smooth little stick closer than ever. He felt sure that if he dropped it he would go to the earth with a bump that would give him a severe headache; for surely his rise in the world must have had something to do with this shining thing which gleamed now between his brown, and not very clean, fingers.

He looked at it as he sailed, and suddenly there came to him a remembrance of stories he had heard in the village about fairies—fairies with wands. Yes, every fairy had a wand, and by waving this wand he could go everywhere and get everything he wanted.

"I wonder if I'm a fairy now," muttered Peter, "that I feel so light. Have I got wings, and am I flying?"

He looked over the shoulder of his old, brown coat, but there were no signs of wings there.

"Still, this must be a wand," said Peter to himself, "and I'll see if I can get anything with it."

The earth had vanished completely now, so he held out the silver stick and said, "I'm tired of standing up. I wish I had a nice, soft cloud to sit on."

No sooner had he made the wish than a lovely cloud floated toward him. It looked like a bank of swansdown. He climbed into it and sank luxuriously into the softness and lay there and wondered, looking at his shining treasure.

While he was musing he became conscious that he was not alone on the cloud; and raising himself on his elbow he looked down to the next terrace of fleecy white, and there sat the most charming little fairy you would care to see. Peter noticed at once that she carried a wand like his own, and that her wings, so thin and airy, yet looked strong enough to carry her slight figure.

She smiled up at him. "I'm so glad I found you, Peter," she said in a sweet voice. "I told Rose-Petal that I was sure I could, and that you would be glad to bring back her wand."

"Who is Rose-Petal?" asked Peter, gazing admiringly at his companion, who certainly could not have looked prettier anywhere than she did on that pure, fleecy-white cloud bank.

"Rose-Petal is the fairy who owns the wand you have. She lost it last night at a fire-fly ball, and though the fire-flies were very kind and held their lanterns and flew about looking everywhere they could think of, they couldn't find it. Rose-Petal is down beside the dusty road, now, where it is so hot that she feels as if she were wilting; so I know you won't keep her waiting."

The fairy sent another sweet and coaxing smile up at Peter but he frowned.

"It's queer that a fellow can't get away from people even if he climbs up on a cloud miles away from the earth," he said; for the last thing he was willing to do was to give back the wand to Rose-Petal.

"How did you find me?" he added, "and what is your name?"

"My name is Lily-bud, and I found you very easily, only I must say that if I had not seen Rose-Petal's wand in your hand I would have thought it was the wrong person."

"Well, it is the wrong person," said Peter crossly. "This wand is mine."

The fairy nodded sadly. "O, yes," she replied, "I see the Wise Woman was right. She said you told lies!"

"You want to be careful how you talk to me," said Peter very loud, and growing red in the face. "A little more and I'll knock you off this cloud."

Lily-bud laughed, and I can't tell you how pretty she looked when she laughed, because her tiny face had the sweetest dimple in one cheek and her blue eyes laughed, too.

Her gauzy wings opened and closed as a butterfly's will when it is resting on a flower.

"What difference would that make, you poor Peter?" she said.

Peter scowled because her manner and her words made him feel even smaller than she was.

"How did you find me, anyway?" he growled.

"O, I went to the Wise Woman under the hill. We fairies always go to her when we have a hard question; and we never had a harder one than this, for Rose-Petal is the first fairy I ever knew to lose her wand."

Lily-bud's smile vanished and Peter saw her lip tremble.

"Think of her down there, huddling near the root of a big tree. Supposing someone should step on her!"

"Why doesn't she fly up to a safe place then?" asked Peter sullenly. Lily-bud's lip might tremble all it wanted to, he was not going to give up his precious, shiny stick.

"Because without her wand her wings won't work," explained Lily-bud.

"What did that old, stupid Wise Woman tell you?" asked Peter. He was very cross at being found.

"She told me that Peter had found the wand and that he was the sort of boy who would not be willing to give it back, no matter how much Rose-Petal suffered."

Peter laughed. "She is a wise old thing, then," he said.

"I told her I couldn't believe it, for didn't all boys take care of girls? She said no, not all boys, and that Peter was one of the worst. He teased girls and hurt them and so he was a coward. He teased animals and hurt them and so he was a coward. He robbed the eggs out of birds' nests, and threw stones at the birds with a slingshot, and so he was a coward. He kicked his own dog that loved him, and so he was a coward."

Peter listened to all this and grew so hot and angry that he couldn't speak. Besides the anger, there was a very uncomfortable feeling in his breast. It came from the look of disgust in Lily-bud's eyes as they were fixed on him without any fear.

"If you were washed," she said, "and your shoes blacked, you wouldn't be bad looking. I should never think, just to look at you, that you were such a poor wretch."

Peter felt scarlet from head to foot.

"Once more," said Lily-bud. "I'll ask you once more to think of beautiful, bright Rose-Petal suffocating beside the dusty road, and ask you to give back her wand."

Peter was so ashamed that his ears burned and he couldn't meet Lily-bud's eyes, but he shook his head.

Lily-bud, without another word, rose lightly to the tips of her dainty toes, spread her gauzy wings, and flew off the cloud and was soon out of sight.

Peter was glad she was gone. What difference did it make to him what was thought of him by two fairies and an old crone of a Wise Woman? He had the wand. That was the main thing; for he had power now to do what he pleased, and the thing he was most anxious to do was to pay back Lawrence for interfering with him and spoiling his fun.

He waved the wand now and asked to go back to earth. He rose to the tips of his coarse shoes and at once floated gently off the cloud and began the descent.

The pleasant, cool air fanned him and seemed to bear him up on the charming journey. Soon the earth came into view and after awhile he began to recognize familiar objects, and after a bit he alighted at the very spot from which he had arisen.

"I like flying," he said to himself. "I shall do that every day."

Pat was running about, nosing the ground and peering into every nook and cranny in wonder where his master had disappeared. Had Pat been a boy he would have been very glad to have such a master disappear and would hope never to see him again; but dogs are different. Is it any wonder they are called the friends of man, when such treatment as Pat received cannot destroy their affection? One should be most kind to such faithful creatures. Don't you think so?

Well, Peter walked along in a very lordly way, feeling as if he owned the earth, and twirling the little stick that twinkled in the sunlight, and which was going to make him succeed in everything he wanted to do. He gave no thought to Rose-Petal hiding herself, dusty and forlorn, between the tree roots so that no one should step on her.

Pat recognized him and approached timidly and slowly, looking at his master out of the tops of his eyes.

"Hello, Pat," said Peter in the height of his good nature, and with a bound the happy dog was beside him, even daring to give one little jump up on him to tell him how glad he was that Peter wasn't lost.

He looked at the stick and wondered if his master was going to throw it for him to chase; but no, indeed, Peter would run no such risk of losing the wand.

"Besides," he thought, and the thought made him laugh, "if Pat should pick up this stick, he might float up into the sky and live with the dog-star forever, for he wouldn't know enough to ask to come down."

It made Pat so happy to hear his master laugh that he frolicked about as if he had never heard an unkind word in his life.

Peter even began humming a tune as he walked along, still twirling the stick. The forest bordered the road, and his eye caught sight of a handsome red-winged blackbird swinging on a bough. His eyes gleamed. It was such a beauty. He hurriedly picked up a stone.

"Hit the mark, Stone," he ordered gaily, and threw it with sure aim. In a minute he would have those wings to stick in his cap.

He ran forward toward the tree, when a wonderful thing happened. That little stone turned around in the air, and flying back at Peter struck him on the cheek with such a smart blow that a tiny trickle of blood ran down.

"Who did that? Who did that?" cried Peter, thinking at once of Lawrence and looking all around. He struck at Pat, but the dog avoided the blow.

The bird flew swiftly away, singing, "Foolish Peter, Foolish Peter," as he went.

It astonished the boy to understand the bird's song, but he was still so busy hunting for Lawrence, dodging behind some tree, that he did not pay much attention to it. Everything that happened to him lately was strange.

He walked along the road, his hand to his cheek. After awhile he came to the village square where the horse pond was. Many children he knew were there, and among them Lawrence.

"Aha, you ran faster than I did," muttered Peter, "but I will get even with you all the same."

Pat felt his mood, and came sedately after him, his tail hanging limply close to his hind legs.

Peter waved his shining wand and said, "I want Lawrence ducked in the horse pond," and he set himself to laugh at the other boy when he should see him struggling in the pond.

Instantly there was a splash, but it was Peter who was floundering in the water, choking and coughing and making great ado because he couldn't swim.

The children all gathered around, and because each of them had some unpleasant memory of Peter, they laughed even while some of them tried to help him. He was a funny object, kicking and spluttering and clutching the water, with his hair in his eyes.

"Here, Peter, hang on," said Lawrence, and bracing himself by holding to a post, he offered his foot to Peter, who managed to get hold of it and pull himself to the edge where he could climb out.

"Here you, keep out of that pond," said a man coming near and speaking angrily. "Don't you know enough not to try to swim in there?"

Peter crept away, dripping, from the laughter of the children, and Pat followed him close.

"Foolish Peter. Foolish Peter," sang a voice again. This time there was no bird and he thought it sounded like Lily-bud's voice, it was so small and sweet.

"How did I happen to trip and fall in there," the boy wondered as he hurried along.

The worst part of it was being helped out by Lawrence, and Lawrence had laughed too, laughed harder than anybody when Peter was safe on the ground, looking like a drowned rat.

"Foolish Peter," repeated the voice. "You might have made all those children love you, then nobody would have laughed at your troubles."

He hurried along, past the market wagons, and a horse accidentally hit him, turning his head. Peter drew back his foot to kick the horse, as he did Pat; and suddenly he received a kick in his own leg, so severe that it made him jump. He was sure, too, that he heard the horse say: "Foolish Peter," as he shook his head.

The boy hurried the faster, too blind with anger and with the water still dripping from his hair, to care where he was going. He saw that Pat was following on. There was one good thing about Pat. He couldn't laugh, and he couldn't talk and lecture him.

"Where was that Lily-bud, following him and nagging him?" He looked all about, but nothing was to be seen except the country road. His leg ached from the kick he had meant to give the horse, and his clothes stuck to him.

Ahead of him he now saw a huge, coarse bramble bush growing by the side of the road. Peter regarded it eagerly and looked about to see if he had lost the wand in the pond. No, there it was. It had fallen into a side-pocket and was glittering there.

Some one had fired a stone at him, he had tripped and fallen into the horse pond, and somebody hiding under a market wagon had kicked him, but here he was safe. He was the only person on the road, and the thorns on that bramble bush would stop Lawrence's laughing for some time anyway. Peter would sit here close to it by the roadside and laugh at him to his heart's content.

He took out the wand and waved it. "I wish Lawrence was in the middle of that bramble bush," he said.

Suddenly something began to scratch him like a thousand pins and he found himself in the midst of the brambles, which at every move made him squeal as he was scratched in a new place.

Before he managed to get out of that tormenting bush, Peter was a thoroughly frightened and suffering boy. Pat leaped about in distress and even made his own mouth sore trying to pull away the brambles so his master could escape.

At last Peter was free, and rolling to a safe spot on the grass, he set himself to pull out some of the thorns that stuck in his flesh. As he did so Pat licked the hurt places on his master's legs and arms and this, with the sight of the wounds on the dog's own lips, which he had suffered in trying to help Peter, brought tears to the boy's eyes. He put his arms around Pat, and the dog licked his master's cheek in his happiness.

"Wise Peter," said a voice. "Now there is hope."

Peter looked up and there sat Lily-bud swaying on a purple thistle. She smiled very kindly at the boy.

"You've had a hard time, haven't you?" she said.

Peter nodded. He was trying to stop the bleeding of Pat's lips with the edge of his soft, wet shirt. "I wish I had never kicked my dog," he said.

At that Lily-bud's face grew very happy. "Do you begin to see that you didn't understand how to use Rose-Petal's wand?" she asked.

Peter felt too crushed to speak. He shook his head.

"You see," explained Lily-bud, "that wand belongs to a good fairy."

Peter looked up at her and the truth began to come to him slowly. Lily-bud smiled and sat on her purple cushion and swayed, and let him think.

"Then I suppose it would cure Pat's mouth," he said eagerly, at last.

She nodded. "Try it," she answered.

Peter waved the glittering stick in his scratched hand. "I want Pat's mouth to be well," he said, and instantly the dog yawned and licked his chops with satisfaction, for they were as whole and comfortable as ever they were.

Peter gave him a hug. "How about my arms and legs?" he asked then, rather shamefaced.

Lily-bud shook her head. "Pat got his scratches in love," she said; and Peter looked off and began to think some more.

As soon as he dropped his hand from the dog, Pat would tuck his head under it again. It was so wonderful to have his master pet him. He couldn't get enough of it.

"Isn't it strange," said Lily-bud, "how much happiness children are willing to miss by not being kind? Do you think that ducking Lawrence in the pond would give you half as much fun as to see his face if you gave him something nice?"

"I could give him something nice with the wand," replied Peter.

Lily-bud nodded. "Yes," she answered.

Peter was thinking faster than he had ever thought in his life. "But I haven't any right to," he said.

"Why?" asked Lily-bud; but she looked very much pleased.

"Because it doesn't belong to me," he answered, and at this Lily-bud was so happy that she flew right over to him and alighted on his scratched hand.

"You are growing wise, Peter," she said.

"I have a knife that Lawrence thinks is the best one he ever saw," said Peter, "and that is my own to give."

"Right-O," said Lily-bud. "Now who is the next person to think about?" she asked.

Peter's eyes met hers very brightly, and he saw her wings close and unclose in her eagerness. After a moment more of thought he waved the wand once again. "I wish we were with Rose-Petal," he said.

In less time than it takes to tell it, he and Pat found themselves under a large, spreading tree a little away from a roadside, and there, with her tiny hands clinging to the moss, was a lovely fairy who looked over her shoulder at Pat with frightened eyes.

"All right, all right," sang Lily-bud, flitting around Peter's head on bright wings. The moment Rose-Petal heard her friend's voice she turned about. Peter saw that this new fairy's wings were drooping and that she looked pale and sad. He could hardly wait to give her what was her own, and he leaned down, holding out the bright bit of silver.

"Here is your wand, Rose-Petal," he said.

How gladly the little creature seized it, and Peter had the pleasure of seeing her cheeks flush and her eyes grow bright and her gauzy wings lift, while rosy color ran in waves all over her white gown, from which the dust fell away. She looked up at him with lovely, grateful eyes, and flew twice around his head before she alighted on his shoulder and spoke into his ear.

"And what can I do for you, Peter?" she asked in a voice that was like sweet music. "Your arms are bleeding."

"I don't deserve anything," replied Peter, not daring to move with that dainty being on his shoulder.

"I can't leave you without showing my gratitude," said Rose-Petal, and Lily-bud felt so happy and full of fun that she alighted on Pat's ear, but he thought a twig was tickling him, and he put up his paw so she whirred away laughing, and then flew back to Rose-Petal and took her hand.

"This is a very uncomfortable, wet coat you're standing on," she said.

"I think so too," replied Rose-Petal, "so first we'll forget all those scratches." She touched Peter with the wand and instantly his arms and legs were smooth—"and then," she continued, "we'll make him as nice outside as he is inside." She touched him again and all the shabby clothes were gone, and the boy found himself dressed in a fine, strong suit with shoes that fitted him perfectly.

"Good bye, Peter," she said, "and if I ever lose my wand again I hope you will be the one to find it."

There was a little, whirring sound, Peter's cheek was fanned by a zephyr, and the fairies were gone. He called them, for he wanted to thank Rose-Petal, but there was no reply.

When, later, he and Pat came walking home they created some excitement on the street and in his cottage.

"I said that boy would come to no good," said one old woman who saw him pass. "Let some one fetch the constable. He has stolen a new suit of clothes and should be clapped in jail."

His mother questioned him and he told her that a fairy gave him the clothes and that he had been in the sky on a cloud.

"Poor child, he has had a sunstroke," exclaimed his mother, and she put him to bed and nursed him for a couple of days, but when he arose the new clothes were still there, and he put them on and went back to school.

Little by little the girls and boys found they need not avoid him, and he carried out his plan to give Lawrence the precious knife, and this made Lawrence his friend for life.

Peter was so changed and quiet and thoughtful that many of the grown people who heard what he had told his mother said that he had lost his mind; but the school teacher, who had suffered much from his pranks, in the past, shook her head.

"No indeed," she said earnestly. "He has found it. Watch and see if Peter doesn't come to be the happiest boy in the village."

And sure enough he did.

CHAPTER VI.

THE GOLDEN KEY.

The next time Lois and Hal asked Wenonah for a story she said she had noticed how happy they seemed to be together and that they made her think of a little brother and sister she knew of who lived in a far country where the rivers had very long names.

"Will you tell us about them?" asked Lois, as she and Hal settled themselves to work on their baskets.

"Yes," replied Wenonah. "This special river that I am thinking of was named Wapsipinicon." Her eyes sparkled at the children as she said it, for she knew that name was a mouthful.

"Whew!" exclaimed Hal, "I'd have to practice a week to say that word."

"Well, if you had seen this river," went on Wenonah, "you wouldn't have cared what its name was, it was so lovely. It did not run very swiftly, but dreamed along between its flowery banks like a maiden who strolls in pleasant paths, musing as she goes.

The water was so clear you could see the fish swimming in it, and the gold-brown sand at the bottom. The rocks that peeped out here and there made little whirlpools and waterfalls as the river gurgled around them.

This brother and sister loved each other so much they never thought of quarreling. Where you saw one you would be pretty sure to find the other. They were very fond of playing on the river bank because the best wild flowers grew there and when their work was done around their home they would run a race every day to see which would get into the woods first, and then, crashing through the bushes and between the big trees, they would scamper until they came out into the sunshine again by the river.

They loved that beautiful playmate, the river, always running away, yet always there, whispering and laughing and welcoming them with every sunny ripple.

One afternoon the children espied a new flower of a deep orange color growing on a high bank near a clump of bushes. When they reached the blossom they found that it gave off a delicious spicy odor. They were delighted and stooped eagerly to pick it, but before their hands reached the stem a clear little voice spoke severely.

"What is your name, little boy?"

The two stood close together in their surprise and did not answer.

The voice spoke again. "What is your name, little boy?"

"My name is Pierre," answered the boy, looking all about for his questioner.

"What is your name, little girl?" asked the voice.

It was such a sweet voice, as well as shrill, that the little girl was not really afraid, but she stood a little closer to her brother.

"My name is Iona," she said.

Then Pierre spoke quickly, "But who are you?"

"I am one of the guards of the fairy queen," was the reply; and suddenly the children saw the owner of the shrill little voice.

He was about as tall as your finger, dressed in green so exactly the color of the bush on which he was standing that no wonder they had not seen him sooner. A sword hung by his side, and looking closely they saw that it was a thorn. An acorn cup was his cap, and stuck in it was a tiny stiff feather some bird had dropped.

He was so cunning Iona longed to pick him up, but he looked so important and stern she felt sure that he would resent any attack on his dignity with that very sharp sword, and she thought she would better let him alone.

"That orange flower," went on the guard, "belongs to the fairy king and queen and you must not break it."

"Do they own all these wild-flowers?" asked Pierre. "I have picked a lot of them. We didn't know they belonged to anybody."

"No, their flower garden is not like that of mortals, all huddled together in one place," (the guard spoke quite scornfully). "Their flowers are scattered and that is why they require guards. Some are in the woods, some in the mountains, some in ravines, so now you understand, unless you are very dull mortal children."

"O, we understand," returned Iona eagerly. "Do you suppose we could see the fairy king and queen? We have wanted to all our lives."

The guard lifted his little shoulders and looked very proud. "It is possible," he said, "but not the easiest thing in the world."

"We wouldn't care if it was very hard indeed," said Pierre earnestly. "Is that thorn of yours instead of a wand?"

"I don't know what you mean by a thorn," returned the guard, and Iona noticed that he looked displeased.

"He means your sword, please, Sir," she said, so very humbly that the guard's face cleared, and she gave Pierre's hand a tight squeeze to remind him that sometimes the smaller people are the bigger they feel themselves to be.

"No, I don't need any wand. My duty is simply to keep order. I have nothing to do with helping other people about their affairs as Rose-Petal and Lily-bud and others like them are always doing."

Iona tried not to laugh. The guard was so small and thought so much of himself.

"If I should pick this orange flower what would happen to me?" asked Pierre. "Would you take me before the king and queen?" He was thinking that might be a good way to get there.

"It would be my duty to thrust your fingers through and through," replied the guard, his hand on his sword hilt and his face very threatening, "and you should never see the king and queen."

"Oh, we wouldn't do it, of course," exclaimed Iona hastily, "since you ask us not to, and if you would be so very kind as to tell us how to get to the fairy court we couldn't thank you enough."

The guard's fierce frown vanished and he regarded the children more cheerfully.

"First," said he, "of course you would have to travel some distance."

"O yes," they cried.

"You will have to do exactly as I tell you."

"Of course," the answer came very eagerly.

"You, Pierre," said the guard fairy, "must think of a number. You, Iona, must think of a letter. Be sure not to forget them. Then when I tell you what to do you must each get on them, one on the letter and one on the number and sail across the Wapsipinicon. On the opposite bank you will find a pool lying in the midst of bulrushes. That is a fairy pool and there you will meet a sentry called Bullfrog. He will ask your names and your business and you must tell him what you are seeking and he will help you on your way. As soon as you get on your letter and number I will push you off from the bank with my sword and you will have a safe journey."

"O let us go at once," cried the children.

The guard looked very strange for a moment. "It is so long since I helped mortals to go to the fairy court that I have forgotten something," he said slowly. "The last children that went to court did a dreadful thing and I had forgotten it. I don't believe you will be able to go after all."

"Tell us what it was," begged Pierre. "How could anything other children did keep us from going?"

"Why they lost the key to the palace gate," said the guard. "Of course fairies don't need it, but mortals do. You can not enter without it."

Pierre and Iona looked at one another. This was surely a hard situation.

"There is no harm in our hunting for the key, is there?" asked Iona.

"No," returned the guard, "No harm, and no hope. You must know that many people have searched for it."

"Let us try at any rate," said Pierre. "If we should find the key and come back may we call you?"

"I'm a very busy person," said the guard, "for as you can understand I have to follow children about from place to place. However, if you find the key you may come back here and standing in the same spot say,

'Come, brave flower-guard, near or far,

Wapsipinicon, 'rah, 'rah, 'rah!'

and I will be with you."

The guard held himself very straight.

"What does the key look like?" asked Iona.

"It is small and made of gold," said the guard.

"Thank you so much," cried both the children, but they found they were talking to a green bush. The guard had vanished.

The orange flower was sending out such charming fragrance that they looked at it once more, wistfully, then at each other, and shook their heads.

"We said we wouldn't, you know," said Iona.

"Besides," returned Pierre, "we have to find that key or else never see the fairy court. Those children must have dropped it in the woods or in the water, for if it had been on the grass it could easily have been found."

Brother and sister stood hand in hand on the bank of the river, wondering if somewhere amid its golden sand lay a little golden key.

"Do you remember," said Iona, "what the flower guard said about two fairies who helped people with their affairs? I was thinking how nice it would be if one of them would help us now. Do you remember their names?"

"Yes, I think they were Rose-bud and Lily-petal."

"Let us see if we can persuade them to come," said Iona. "The flower guard gave us a rhyme for himself. Can you make a verse about Rose-bud?"

Pierre thought deeply for a moment. "I don't believe I can," he answered. "Can you? You must, Iona. It's necessary."

So Iona thought and thought. At last she said,

"Rose-bud of the gauzy wing,

We need you like anything."

Then the children looked all about. The forest trees back of them were waving and shimmering in the sun. Daises and buttercups were bright along the shore, and a tangle of wild rose-bushes covered with blossoms made the air sweet; but no fairy appeared.

"They must be good fairies," said Pierre, "or else they wouldn't help people, and there must be some way to get them. That proud little flower guard appeared to us quick enough without any verse being said to him."

"Perhaps we haven't the names right," said Iona. "I wonder if it wasn't Lily-bud and Rose-Petal."

"Try again, then," returned Pierre.

So Iona thought very earnestly again and at last said,

"Rose-Petal bright, Rose-Petal gay,

Help us to find the key today."

"What key, children?" asked a voice, and turning quickly they saw on the nearest wild rose-bush a fairy swaying. Rosy waves swept over her white gown in ripples of color, and her wings changed from silver to rose as they closed and unclosed.

Pierre and Iona hurried toward her.

"O dear Rose-Petal," said Iona, clasping her hands in happiness at seeing the bright little being. "The flower guard will help us to the fairy court if we can only find the key to the palace gate. Some children lost it. Can you help us?"

Rose-Petal shook her head and smiled. "I will do what I can, but when mortals lose things, mortals must find them."

"But I suppose you know everything," said Pierre. "I suppose you know where the key is."

"No," returned Rose-Petal, "I don't know where it is, but I shall be glad if you find it, for it is rather a pity children should not be able any longer to visit our court."

"Do you go there often?" asked Pierre.

"I live there," replied Rose-Petal. "I am one of the queen's maids of honor."

"Then why can't you take us?" suggested Iona eagerly.

"You know already," returned the fairy. "Mortals must use the key, and when two children like you, who are not selfish or quarrelsome, wish to go I am glad to help them for they already have the greatest key of all, the key that unlocks all earthly doors."

"What is that?"

"Love," replied Rose-Petal, "and for that reason they will not carry into the fairy court anything but love. Many children have too much other baggage to carry: selfishness, bad temper, sometimes even dishonesty. That was the trouble with the last mortal visitors we had, and it was in some quarrel that they lost the key. Now this is what I will do for you." Rose-Petal produced two acorn cups such as the flower guard had worn. "Here are two caps. They have many virtues and will make you understand much that you never understood before."

She touched the children with her silver wand. The children took the acorn cups gratefully, but they smiled at each other and then at the pretty face and bright eyes of the fairy.

"I don't see how we can ever wear such caps as these," said Iona, laughing.

Rose-Petal smiled. "They will fit you when you put them on," she said. "Try it."

The children placed the little caps on the top of their heads and suddenly the strangest thing happened to Rose-Petal. She grew as big as they were, and Pierre and Iona were so occupied with that change that they did not notice that the new caps fitted them perfectly.

Rose-Petal with the vibrant waves of rose color playing over her wings and her gauzy gown, looked so tall and dignified and beautiful that Iona wondered how a minute ago she could have longed to take her up in her hand.

"I didn't know there were such large fairies," exclaimed Pierre.

Rose-Petal laughed gaily. "And I didn't know there were such small children," she answered, and at once there was nothing where she had been standing but a huge wild rose. Pierre and Iona grasped each other's hands. They were swinging on the bough of a bushy tree with giant roses all around them.

"How did we get up in this tree?" asked Iona.

"I suppose we climbed up," said Pierre, "but I don't remember it. Shall I help you down?" He took off his cap to put it in his pocket because he knew it was valuable to them in some way, and instantly he was standing beside the wild rose-bush, and there before him was a little creature no bigger than Rose-Petal standing on a twig and wearing an acorn cap.

He laughed and took the cap off his sister's head and at once she stood beside him on the ground, beside the rose-bush.

"Why, Pierre!" she cried.

"Why, Iona," he answered. "Our caps are wonderful things, but I don't see yet how they are going to help us."

"We shall find out," replied Iona. "First of all I think we ought to search the river, don't you?"

"That would take us the rest of our lives," returned Pierre, "for the river begins in the mountains and flows into the sea."

"But the water-nixie will perhaps know," said Iona. "Rose-Petal believed there was hope of our finding the key or she would not have helped us. Her eyes looked kind. She wouldn't play tricks."

"No," returned Pierre, "I'm sure she was a good fairy. Then you will have to make up another verse, Iona."

"You do this one," suggested his sister.

Pierre scratched his head and wrinkled his forehead but rhymes wouldn't come, so Iona tried again.

They both stood close to the river and Pierre said, "I think our caps might help. Rose-Petal said we should understand everything better."

So, pushing the acorn cups down over their heads again they found they fitted perfectly and suddenly the river had become such a great torrent that they stepped back a little and Iona cried in a high, sweet voice,

"Wapsipinicon, 'rah, 'rah, 'rah,

Come, pretty Nixie, wherever you are."

Instantly the waterfall formed by the largest rock that stuck out of the river bed became misty, and a spray rose from it, higher, higher, higher, until the children saw a lovely maiden's form grow clearer and clearer.

The crystal water shimmered over her head and long hair and gown of mist, and she stood, a slender, lovely, dripping fountain and gazed upon the tiny children kindly.

"It is very good of you to come," said Pierre. He snatched off his cap politely and nearly stepped upon Iona, who leaped away from him. He restored it very quickly you may be sure, and the Nixie continued to gaze at them through her rippling, watery veil, without apparently noticing these extraordinary changes.

"We are searching for the lost key to the fairy palace gate," explained Iona. "It is of gold. Have you seen it glittering in your river?"

"No," returned the Nixie in a gurgling tone. "The key is not in the river."

"Do you know where it is?" cried Pierre eagerly.

"Those of the ground must tell you," gurgled the Nixie. "The water knows nothing of it."

The springing fountain lowered slowly, slowly, the mist melted and the waterfall played as before over its sturdy rock.

The children looked at one another. "That was good," said Pierre. "It saves a great deal of time. We can go faster without our caps, since Rose-Petal forgot to give us wings to go with them, and next we must go to the forest."

They took off the caps and hurried fast as their feet would carry them back into the woods.

"Now, slow and sure," said Pierre, and they fitted on their caps again. They saw at once what Rose-Petal had meant by what she said of their being better able to understand, for to their great surprise a bird, who had begun to twitter as they stepped in among the trees, was speaking.

"There are those two children again," she chirped. "They crash through the bushes here so many times a day it is very strange they never seem to remember that trees were made for us and not for them. I'm always expecting them to look up and see my nest, and some children are robbers, you know."

"We are not," cried Iona, but the bird flew away, paying no attention to her and singing as she went, "Robbers, robbers," to warn the other birds.

"I can't bear to have them think that," said Iona with tears in her eyes.

"No matter now," said Pierre, "we must look steadily at the ground as we walk to see if we can find that key."

A bird up among the highest branches had heard Iona's words of grief that she should be thought a robber and he felt sorry for her.

"Ask the Wise Man," he sang.

"Where is he?" cried Pierre.

"Downstairs, downstairs," sang the bird, as he too, flew away.

"How can there be stairs in the woods?" asked Pierre.

"In the hollow tree,

See what you can see,"

sang somebody. It might have been a bird, but the children thought it sounded like Rose-Petal's voice. At any rate they began looking for a hollow tree and at last found one.

They climbed up with their small hands and feet and looked all about the hollow. At one side there seemed to be a dark hole and as they came closer they saw little stairs leading downward.

A woodpecker outside the trunk saw them go in. Tapping hard on the bark he said, "Flatter him, flatter him."

"I don't see anyone to flatter," said Pierre.

"Nor I, but perhaps we shall," returned Iona. "Let us go down those stairs. The birds know all about the woods and we would better obey them."

So they started down the dark flight of stairs which wound down, down, between the twisted roots of trees that had a very earthy smell.

At last they came out into a sort of room, a room with no shape at all, you might say, because there were so many passages leading off from it; but it was large enough for the little brown man who stood there looking with surprise to see visitors appearing from the stairway. He had a long white beard, but his face looked like a potato, Iona thought, his eyes were so small, and his color, clothes and all, so brown.

The place was lighted by glow worms that hung from the top of the room and there was a table that was an old tree root, and a chair of the same.

"Flatter him, flatter him," the woodpecker had advised, and Iona wondered how anyone could flatter such a droll being, as homely and earthy as he could be.

"Be sure to keep your cap on," whispered Pierre. "We should bump our heads dreadfully if we lost them, and never get out, either."

The little man did not look glad to see them.

"If you have come to get employment I don't need any more helpers," he said, "so you may as well go right back. This is going to be a very busy day with me. I felt thunder a minute ago."

"How can you feel thunder?" asked Pierre.

"You don't even know that?" said the little man, "and yet you thought you could work for me!"

Iona, with the necessity for flattery still on her mind, here spoke:

"Of course we don't expect to know a quarter as much as you do," she said earnestly. "We are only children, and upstairs they call you the Wise Man."

The gnome (for that is what he was), stroked his beard, and his eyes shone with satisfaction. "Of course. They naturally would," he said. "What else could they call me?"

"O, what darling kittens," cried Iona, stooping to some little dark objects she saw on the ground near the table, and she smoothed the delicate, dainty fur. "O Pierre, did you ever feel anything so soft?"

The gnome stroked his beard again. It was a way he had when he was pleased. "You are certainly very ignorant," he said. "It is a good thing you came down here to learn a few things. Those are not kittens, they are moles."

"Why, so they are," said Pierre, "and would you mind telling us, Sir, what you meant by feeling the thunder? Where we live, we hear it."

"Why it shakes the earth, of course, and when I feel it vibrating all around me I know I shall soon be busy unless the storm passes around. You'd better get out now, for when the rain falls I shall have no time to teach you anything more and I can't employ such ignorant children as you are."

"Would you mind telling me what your workmen do?" asked Pierre. "You seem to be all alone."

"Somebody must be here to give directions, of course."

"Certainly, Sir," said Pierre, "but my sister and I don't know much about what happens under the ground and it is so interesting to hear."

"Who did you suppose carried the water to the roots of the trees and flowers?"

"We didn't know, Sir."

"Who did you suppose helped the new little rootlets to find a drink, and guided them to the softest earth-places so they could reach down and eat and grow strong?"

"We didn't know, Sir."

"Well, you know now. Do you see all those passages leading off in every direction from this room?"

"Yes, Sir."

"They are full of my workmen for miles around. They have all felt the thunder and they are ready."

"That is very wonderful," said Iona, who had risen from caressing the moles and was listening attentively. "You know, then, everything that is in the ground, don't you?"

"Certainly I do!"

"Do you know what is on top of the ground? We are searching for a golden key—"

"O, that golden key!" exclaimed the gnome. "What a to-do there has been about that key!"

"O, Sir, if you know anything about it," exclaimed Pierre, "do tell us. The birds told us that you were the Wise Man and sent us down to see you. They felt you could help us."

The gnome nodded slowly, and closed one of his little potato eyes in a knowing wink.

"Trust the birds for that," he said. "They have their own reasons for sending you down here. Anything to make you believe the key was on the ground, or in it."

"Are you sure it isn't, dear Mr. Wise Man?" asked Iona.

"Perfectly sure. We go upstairs in the twilight when the sun won't hurt our eyes. We know everything that lies on the ground in this forest."

"And the key isn't there?" asked Pierre.

"Do you know where it is—you who know everything?" cried Iona, grasping the edge of the gnome's earthy smock with beseeching hands.

"I know everything that it is my business to know," returned the gnome impatiently, "and that is enough. Begone, now. O, the birds," he added with another knowing nod and wink, "Leave it to the birds. Out with you! The rain is coming."

"But we'd like to stay here until the shower passes," suggested Pierre.

"No indeed. I must get to my work and command my army. How do I know that you would not make off with a glowworm or a mole? Have you brought any references?"

The children were forced to admit that they had not, so the gnome hustled them up the stairs and they climbed until they came out into the daylight of the hollow tree.

A flash of lightning greeted them, and they laughed as they cuddled down into the powdered dead wood in the depths of the hollow and watched the silver rain which at once began to fall, and listened to the grand peals of thunder that seemed to shake the foundations of the earth.

"It's no wonder he could feel the thunder," said Pierre.

"Did you speak to me?" asked a laughing voice. It sighed even as it laughed, like a breeze passing through the tops of the trees.

The children looked all about.

"Pierre, you made a rhyme," exclaimed Iona. "'You were a poet and didn't know it' and we know by this time that fairies love poetry. Something lovely is near us. Do you suppose a dryad lives in this tree?"

The thunder seemed to rip the clouds apart and the fast-falling silver rain began to be lighted by an occasional sunbeam. Iona looked very happy and excited and she held Pierre's hand tightly while she said:

"Lovely dryad of the wood,

Help us, if you'll be so good."

Instantly, with a swirl of green draperies, a slender, laughing girl stood before them. The rain sent its silver lances over her golden hair and leaf green gown without wetting her in the least.

"You are making yourself very much at home," she said with a gay little ripple of laughter that clothed all she said.

"We didn't know it was your tree," said Pierre, his hand going up to his cap —but he remembered in time and dropped the hand. "We went downstairs to see the Wise Man because we are hunting for the key to the gate of the fairy palace, and he thinks the birds know more about it than they tell."

"My birds, my birds," sighed the dryad.

"Of course they are!" exclaimed Iona. "You'll show us where to go, won't you?"

"Secrets, secrets," laughed the dryad, a very mischievous look in her pretty eyes.

"But what possible use can a key be to a bird?" asked Pierre.

"Ask them, ask them," sang the dryad.

"No, no," exclaimed Iona, "the birds think we are robbers when we wouldn't rob them for the world, and yet if we take the key from them they might call it robbing. What shall we do?" She clasped her hands together and the dryad, mischievous as she was, and full of fun, appeared to feel some sympathy with her. At any rate the green-clad maiden leaned forward, and with a hand as white as mist touched one of Iona's golden curls.

"Fair exchange," she sighed, laughing. "Fair exchange is no rob—" her voice died away, and with the voice, her leaf-like gown and fair face.

"I've heard that before about fair exchange," said Pierre. "Iona, we will let all the birds know that you will give a curl for the key. I believe the dryad has helped us more than anyone."

The rain ceased and the children climbed out of their hollow, and hand in hand walked among the dripping trees. The sun burst forth from the racing clouds, and the birds, flying from their shelters among the branches, began to sing.

"There are those children again," sang one.

"Why should you be afraid of creatures as small as we are?" sang another.

"And we love you so, we love you so," cried Iona.

The first bird heard this. He was a wood-thrush. "Do you think we can believe that?" he asked of his friend, who was a vireo.

"It is as well to watch them," said the vireo. "I lost some eggs once."

"Listen to them," said the wood-thrush. "They are trying to sing, too."

"Birds of air, O, list to me,

I am searching for a key

Golden as the silky curl

Growing on this little girl.

If you'll give the key to me

I'll give you the curl, you see;

Curls are soft and are the best

Lining for a cozy nest."

The children walked on slowly, singing their song, and one bird called to another to listen, until a flock flitted from tree to tree, following them and looking down with bright eyes at Iona's golden curls.

At last a larger bird joined the throng. As soon as he heard the children's song and took a good look at Iona's golden hair he flapped his wings and made a great outcry. He was a magpie and a great talker at all times, but now he shrieked at the top of his lungs.

"A hawk! A hawk! Fly, Fly!" and all the other birds fled away with the speed of arrows.

As soon as they were out of sight the magpie flew down to Iona.

"Go no further," he said, and his eyes shone as a sunbeam glinted on Iona's curls. "I have your key. Do you mean what you said about the curl?"

"O yes, Mr. Magpie," cried the children.

"Then I can bite it off right now," said the magpie, "and carry it up to my tree when I go to get the key, which is woven into the side of my nest."

Iona put her head down obediently, but Pierre stepped in front of her.

"No, Mr. Magpie," he said firmly. "Fair exchange is no robbery. Let us see the key, first."

The bird, seeing that it was of no use to try to get the curl and keep the key too, flew away. It was not very long before he returned with a bit of shining metal in his beak. It proved to be a beautifully carved little key, bright as a sunbeam, and Iona held it in both hands while putting her head down to let the magpie choose a curl. As she did so, her acorn cap fell off, and no cry of hawk ever made a bird fly away faster than that magpie flew from the big little girl.

"O, what a pity!" said Iona, nearly crying. "The birds will think worse of us than ever."

"No," returned Pierre, taking off his own cap, and standing beside her, "it is good luck for the magpie, for he will get a big curl now, instead of a little one. I see him up there now, chattering away in the top of that big oak."

Pierre took his knife out of his pocket and choosing a curl in the back of Iona's head, where its loss would not be much noticed, he cut it off and hung it over a bush, where it shone like gold.

Then the children hurried away and hid behind a tree where they watched until they saw the magpie fly down, seize the curl, and fly off swiftly.

So then with light hearts the children went back through the woods and out again upon the river bank.

"Do you remember the number you chose, Pierre?"

"Yes. Do you remember your letter?"

"Yes," returned Iona joyously, and they ran up the bank towards the orange flower.

"Come, little flower-guard, near or far,

Wapsipinicon, 'rah, 'rah, 'rah."

shouted Pierre, but though they hunted all over the bush no little, green-clad fairy appeared. The children looked at one another blankly. What if now that they had the precious key, the guard failed to keep his promise?

Suddenly Pierre laughed. "It is our fault," he said, recalling the proud and important look of the guard. "He doesn't know that he is small. I remember now what he told us," so Pierre called,

"Come, brave flower-guard, near or far,

Wapsipinicon, 'rah, 'rah, 'rah."

and at once the guard with his flashing eye, his green uniform, and with his hand on the hilt of his sword, stood before them.

"Look!" cried Iona, showing the key. "It was woven into the side of a magpie's nest. I gave him one of my curls for it."

The guard seemed pleased and nodded. "You have done well," he said, "and now if you remember your letter and number we will be off."

"Wouldn't it be more convenient if we were your size?" asked Pierre.

"What do you mean by size?" asked the guard frowning.

"My cap is gone!" cried Iona.

Pierre looked all about in his pockets. "So is mine," he returned, looking very blank. "Rose-Petal gave us some caps like yours—" he was explaining, but the guard interrupted him.

"This is not Rose-Petal's affair, it is mine, so don't ask any more foolish questions but follow me."

They went down to the river's edge, and there were the letter and the number, dancing on the ripples like little rafts, and the children got on board.

"You remember my directions?" asked the guard.

"Perfectly," they replied. Then the guard with the point of his sword pushed the rafts off from shore and waved them adieu.

They called back their thanks to him and began to enjoy their ride very much. They could see the fish swimming about them, and several times they thought the fish gently nosed their rafts along so the current could not bear them down stream.

At last they touched the opposite shore and jumping out they looked about for the pool. The bulrushes were so thick that for some time they could not find it, but at last they saw another orange flower like the first, flaming among the green and they hastened their steps. Its odor perfumed all the air.

"Do you suppose we may pick this one?" asked Iona, when a deep, gruff voice suddenly exclaimed, "Chug! Stand ho! Who are you?"

Then the children saw that they were on the edge of the pool and on a near rock sat the biggest bullfrog they had ever seen.

"We were hunting for you, Sir Bullfrog," said Pierre politely.

"Chug! chug!" said the frog, and his white throat swelled as he said it.

Then Pierre told him their experiences and that the flower-guard had promised them that the frog would take them to the palace.

"Let me see where the curl was cut off. Chug! chug! And let me see the key. Chug! chug!" returned the frog, without moving.

So Iona bowed her head and her curls fell thick on either side with a little cropped lock of hair in the middle. Then she took the key from the bosom of her dress, for after finding they had lost their acorn caps she wanted to be very,

very careful, so had hid it there.

Then at last the frog was satisfied.

"Fetch your rafts," he said, "and we will be off."

So the children ran back to the riverside and pulled their letter and number out of the water, and placing them on their heads, marched back to the pool.

"Place the letter on my back and the number on that, and then get on yourselves."

"Isn't that a very heavy load for you?" asked Iona, who believed in kindness to animals.

"Chug! No," exclaimed the frog, "I shall probably forget you are there."

"Please don't," said Iona, "because we can't swim." She believed also in kindness to children and she hoped the frog did.

But the frog began chug-chugging as if he were impatient to be gone, so the children jumped aboard laughing, and off they went, the frog making the water foam with the strokes of his long, strong legs.

The pool had looked to them like a circular small pond, but the frog swam to a narrow opening in the tall rushes, and although these nearly brushed the children off for some way, the water widened out again.

It was a long journey. Three times they twisted and turned through narrow openings, but at last they came into a pretty stream that flowed between flowery, tree-shaded banks, and imagine the children's joy when they saw hundreds of the fragrant orange-colored flowers, growing in profusion.

"O, we must be very near," cried Pierre.

"Chug! chug! we are," said the frog, "and I have made up my mind to let the fishes take you back. I found I couldn't forget you were there."

He swam up to a landing of ivory with ivory steps leading down to the water, and who should be standing on the top step, but Rose-Petal herself.

"Welcome," she said as the children leaped joyously to the shore.

"We can't thank you enough, dear Frog," said Iona.

"Chug!" said the frog, and turning around he swam away again as fast as he could go.

"We must tell you the first thing," said Pierre, "that we lost our caps and we are very sorry. We tried not to be careless."

"You were not careless," answered Rose-Petal, "I took them after you found the key."

This was a great relief to the children, and guided by Rose-Petal they walked through avenues of flowers until they reached a gate of mother-of-pearl. Beyond it they could see flowers and fountains and graceful waving trees, and could hear the singing of birds.

Rose-Petal turned to them and smiled, and pointed with her wand to the golden lock. Iona took out the precious key and with it she unlocked the gate of pearl and they walked in. White doves flew about their heads and lighted on the children's heads and hands, and swans sailed about in a pond clear as emerald.

The palace itself now rose before them and it was of mother-of-pearl, very beautiful in shape, and soft looking, like a tinted cloud.

The children were so full of wonder and happiness that they forgot even Rose-Petal. They walked up the flowery avenue to the ivory steps of the palace and straight up them as if in a delightful dream. They entered and passed between guards like the one they already knew, except that these were dressed in white satin and instead of a sword each carried a stalk of lilies of the valley.

Pierre and Iona walked on, and at last came into the throne room. It was more beautiful than they had dreamed; and the pearl walls and floors had a hundred pale tints of violet, rose and gold.

At the end, on a raised platform, were two thrones, and on one sat the queen in a lovely filmy robe, outside of which a splendid train of ermine-trimmed white satin trailed on the floor. The king, too, was dressed in white satin and silver lace, and both king and queen wore crowns of pearls with a diamond star in the front.

Around them were grouped lovely fairies. The children stood still and gazed. Rose-Petal advanced and fell on one knee before the throne.

"Your majesties, these are the children who found the lost key to the palace gate."

"Let them come near," said the king, and obeying a gesture from Rose-Petal, Pierre and Iona drew near to the wonderful beings they had so longed to see.

They imitated Rose-Petal and fell on their knees, and as the king and queen each held out a hand they kissed them, and it was like kissing flowers.

"Rise, dear children, and tell us your adventures," said the queen. "The key is not to leave the palace, and the children who took it away thought by so doing that they could come to our court at any time they wished. Of course they lost it and we should like to hear how you found it again."

"That is true," said the king. "We wish to hear. Speak on."

So the children told their adventures from the beginning, and the fairies standing about the throne listened with as much interest as the king and queen. Their names, besides Rose-Petal, and Lily-bud whom you already know, were Crystal, Thistle-down, Feather-white and Dewdrop.

When Pierre and Iona had finished their recital the king and queen smiled.

"We are well pleased," said the king. "Will you tell us, Pierre, why you chose One as your number?"

"Yes, your majesty," replied Pierre. "It is because you would be the first king and queen we had ever seen, and we knew you were the one and only fairy king and queen."

"And you, Iona," said the queen. "Why did you choose the letter G?"

"Because, your majesty," replied Iona, "you were a great and good king and queen."

The royal pair smiled again.

"Those were very good reasons," said the queen, "and very pleasant for us to hear. Now my maidens will give you some refreshment before you go, and then you may take, each of you, an orange flower. The name of it is Good Cheer and it will not wither, but bloom forever, making all around you glad with its perfume and brightness."

"After that," added the king, "we desire that you be returned safely to your home in our water chariot, and that your lives be always as happy as they are today."

Upon this the king and queen again held out their hands and the children kissed them and then followed Rose-Petal and her charming sisters out of the throne room.

As the children had no wings the fairies very politely refrained from using theirs and all walked together out into the gardens where they played games and ate delicious fruits and little cakes made of honey and nuts, and drank something delightful, they knew not what it was, from crystal cups.

At last the sun began to sink into the West and the children's eyelids were ready to sink too, from all they had done this wonderful day. They were very, very happy as each gathered an orange flower.

Then Rose-Petal led them out past the emerald pond, with its snowy swans, and the doves again alighted softly on their heads and arms.

Iona turned the key in the palace gate, and they passed through. Then she locked it again. The children took a last look at the little golden key and felt sorry for the children who had carried it away and therefore could never go back again.

They walked on to the bank of the river and there floated a charming, opal shell, with pink velvet cushions, and harnessed to it by rosy ribbons were four swans. Pierre and Iona clapped their hands with joy at the sight.

"Their majesties' own water chariot," said Rose-Petal. "You will have a pleasant journey."

"But must we say good-bye to you, dear Rose-Petal?" asked Iona.

"I will meet you at the Wapsipinicon," she answered with a little nod, and mounting on her bright wings she disappeared into the air.

Pierre and Iona stepped on board the boat and seated themselves on the soft cushions under the opal-colored canopy formed by the curling ends of the lovely shell, and with a smooth motion the swans moved forward, between the flowery banks of the stream.

"It is like being a king and queen ourselves," said Pierre.

"Yes," replied Iona, holding her dear flower close.

In and out, through narrow ways and broad, but all beautiful, the swans swam on. Sometimes drooping trees dipped their tassels in the water, and the air was always sweet.

At last the children began to see bulrushes and they remembered their friend, the frog. Would he come to meet them?

Sure enough, as the stream narrowed and the bulrushes grew more thickly, the swans began to move more and more slowly. At last they stopped.

"Chug! chug!" said a voice. "Stand, ho."

"Dear Mr. Frog, how kind of you!" cried Iona as the frog came alongside, on his back the letter and number just as they had left them.

"Where did you get the flowers?" he asked severely.

"The gift of the king and queen," replied Pierre.

The frog sentry seemed satisfied. The presence of the water chariot was proof of royal favor.

"Chug! Get aboard," he said, so Pierre and Iona rose from their stately pink velvet cushions and jumped over upon the raft.

"Thank you, dear swans," they cried, and watched the graceful creatures turn and start to swim back, drawing after them the tinted boat.

The frog began his strong strokes and soon arrived at his home pool on the bank of which stood Rose-Petal, poised on a bulrush.

"Welcome, little travellers," she said, "now to the river." And Pierre and Iona, after bidding a grateful good-bye to the big frog who chug-chugged a farewell to them, jumped out on shore, and picking up their letter and number, started for the Wapsipinicon.

"Rose-Petal, we love you and we thank you," cried the children as they boarded their rafts on their own dear river.

Rose-Petal smiled and pushed off the little boats with her wand. Then she began to sing;

"Gentle river, bear them lightly,

Wind and wave, sing songs of cheer;

In their hearts may love burn brightly,

And protect them from all fear."

The children stood and threw kisses and waved their hands to the good fairy as the ripples bore them on, and her song grew fainter and fainter.

At last they could see her no longer. They were approaching the shore, and soon scrambled out on a convenient rock. The sun was setting and they hastened through the woods and toward home as fast as they could go. Their mother met them at the door.

"What is that lovely fragrance?" she asked as they kissed her.

"These flowers," returned the children, holding up the orange-colored blossoms, which looked like imprisoned sunshine.

Then they told their mother their adventures and at last Pierre again held up the fragrant flower.

"The name of it is Good Cheer," he explained.

Their mother nodded thoughtfully.

"The fairies knew the best gift to give you," she said. "With good cheer one needs little else."

CHAPTER VII.

THE POLAWEE.

"Don't you know any Indian stories, Wenonah?" asked Lois one day when they were all sitting together in the tent, watching the rain through the open door, just as Pierre and Iona had done in the hollow tree. Lois and Hal wished very much that they could have some such experience in fairy land as had come to those other children; and when they said so the Indian girl smiled.

"You will find out," she said, "that we can all call upon the greatest wonder worker of them all every day right now."

"Who? Who is it?" asked the children.

"It is Love," said Wenonah. "Love settles quarrels. Love makes plain people beautiful. Love brings happiness. Supposing Love were taken out of the faces and actions of your father and mother. What would your lives be like?"

"O well, of course, it couldn't be," said Hal, his eyes growing big with such an awful thought.

"What do you suppose makes the king and queen of Fairyland send Rose-Petal and Lily-bud and the others on their errands of kindness?"

"We don't know," answered Lois.

"Love whispers to them that somebody is in need, of course," explained Wenonah. "You asked me if I didn't know any Indian stories and that made me think of the great chief Pola."

"Please tell us about him," begged Hal.

"Did he have any children?" asked Lois.

"Yes, a little daughter named Polawee. She was the most beloved princess in the world and it was all because Love was her constant companion. If she heard of any children who were sorrowful, or hurt, or unhappy, she went to them at once and did not leave them until they were cheered and the world again seemed a glad place to live in. Her father was a great chief with a crown of feathers, and his face and body decorated with bright paint, but he died and was forgotten, while the gentle Polawee has never been forgotten, nor ever will be in that country where they lived.

The people named a river for her. It was a narrow stream, scarcely more than a creek; for Polawee loved this river and often led a crying child to look into its clear depths, for the child was sure to laugh at such a funny face as looked up from the sparkling water. Then Polawee laughed and the ripples laughed and they were all happy together.

Many years afterward when a village of white people had come to be on this spot where the Princess Polawee lived, a little girl named Rowena used to come and stand on the bridge that crossed the stream. She knew about the Indian maiden for whom it had been named—how kind she was, and how good to everybody.

As she stood looking down into the water one day, two tears splashed into the water.

Rowena had red hair and freckles. She was thin and round-shouldered. The school children teased her and called her Hyena. So her heart was very sore and you can imagine when she leaned over the Polawee today what a reflection she saw, with her bent figure, and her sullen, plain, unhappy face. How she wished the Indian princess were here now to take her part and help her to punish the teasing children. She would like to see them all as unhappy as she was.

"Oh Polawee, Polawee," she exclaimed, and more tears splashed into the stream.

"Yes. Doesn't it seem too bad?" said a pleasant little voice. It seemed to come from the weeping willow growing beside the bridge. Rowena started and looked at the tree dipping its drooping leaves into the water.

"If Polawee saw her river today I think it would make her kind heart ache," went on the voice.

Rowena stopped crying and looked all about. Finally she perceived what she thought were the gauzy wings of a dragon-fly, but as they came nearer she saw that it was a lovely little fairy who stood near her on the railing of the bridge.

The fairy smiled when she saw that the astonished child perceived her. "What is your name?" she asked.

"Rowena," replied the little girl, staring with her sad, tearful eyes.

"A pretty name," said the fairy, and she looked so kind that Rowena shook her head.

"But the children call me Hyena," she said, "and I am bent and homely, with red hair—"

"Hair lighted by the sun," said the fairy.

"And freckles," added Rowena.

"The sun's golden kisses," said the fairy.

Her loving expression warmed Rowena's heart.

"Are you the Princess Polawee?" she asked in awe.

"No," replied the fairy, "my name is Lily-bud; but I know all about the Princess Polawee and I thought perhaps you were crying because her river is so changed from the crystal stream where she brought children to look at their unhappy faces, to make them laugh. The princess would scarcely recognize her river if she saw it now."

"What changed it?" asked Rowena.

"People who didn't love it," replied Lily-bud. "When the village grew up here the people didn't like the river. It once rose and overflowed its banks and washed away their seeds and they began to treat it like an enemy. They threw sticks and stones and mud at it."

"As they do at me," said Rowena. "I know that in the old days unhappy children came and looked into the river until they grew glad, so I come every day and stand here and look into the water, but all I see is the girl they all make fun of. I never thought before of pitying the river," she added. "I'm sorry now that I ever threw mud and stones and sticks into it, as I have done many times."

"Come with me," said Lily-bud, holding out her hand; "I will take you to the land where there are only loving thoughts."

"No," replied Rowena, the sullen look settling over her face again, "I will stay and look into the river, for there I shall see the truth. I see why the others despise me, and I despise them too," she added bitterly.

"But you are not seeing the truth," said Lily-bud. "If you had come in Polawee's day you would have seen a true picture of little Rowena, but in this poor, muddy stream, and bent over as you are when you look into it, there is no truth reflected back."

Lily-bud glanced down at the water. "Poor river Polawee," she added, "I am glad the princess can not see what wrong stories you are telling to the children of this day, and not at all your fault."

She smiled again at the little girl with the swollen eyes.

"Come with me," she said, "where there are no lies." Her expression was very sweet.

"I don't see why you want me," said Rowena, hanging her head.

"Because you need Love," returned Lily-bud, "and we will find it. I am going to give you a rule to remember, to use all your life. It is this: Look up and to the right."

Rowena from habit bent over again and gazed at the twisted, distorted image of herself in the muddy river.

"What did I tell you to do?" asked Lily-bud kindly.

Rowena lifted her head, looked up and to the right and there she saw a cloud, tinted with such lovely colors that they held her gaze.

Lily-bud touched her with her wand and they both floated gently up from the bridge until they rested on that cloud, which was sailing on toward the right.

"How beautiful!" exclaimed Rowena. It was so wonderful to be high above all the things that had made her unhappy, and the colors on their cloud, always changing and each more beautiful than the last, made her heart beat fast. She had always loved brightness and had seen so little. The wide sky itself seemed to lift her. She wondered why she had so seldom looked at it.

As they sailed on Rowena began to hear music, as of a chorus of children singing. How charming it was! How joyful it sounded! She wished it might go on forever. She looked all about to locate the sweet sounds, but could see nothing. The music grew ever louder and fuller, so she knew that they must be approaching it, and at last Rowena saw before her a scene so wonderful that it made her eyes wide with delight.

Lily-bud took her hand and they stepped from the cloud upon the edge of an orchard. Some of the trees bore orange blossoms, some oranges, others a variety of fruits, and on the thick green turf children were skipping hand in hand, in circles, and singing as they went. How fragrant the air was; what brilliant plumage showed as birds flitted from tree to tree urged by the children's songs to break forth in their own melodies.

Rowena clasped her hands and looked at her companion. "What," she asked, "made you leave all this and come to me by the muddy Polawee?"

"Love," replied Lily-bud.

Now the singing children caught sight of the stranger and ceased their music and skipping. There were boys among them, and Rowena feared boys. She shrank and would have hidden behind Lily-bud had she not been so small. Lily-bud saw her expression.

"Remember the rule," she said.

So Rowena, desperately afraid she would be pelted with something, although there seemed only fruit to throw there, looked up and to the right. Sitting among the branches of orange blossoms she saw a white dove, and the dove, seeing her look at him, flew down to her band, and this made Rowena so happy that she didn't care what was done to her if only they wouldn't frighten this lovely white creature away.

"A new child, a new child," cried the children and they ran to meet

Rowena, who put up her other hand to guard the dove, and shrank back.

"Come and sing, come and sing," cried the children. "The dove can sit on your head." And wonderful to relate the white bird immediately flew up and perched on Rowena's red locks, while two children seized her hands and led her into the circle.

"I don't know the song," she said, half-crying with surprise and happiness.

"Yes you do. All children know the song," they told her. "Just open your mouth and it will come out."

And it did come out; and Rowena sang and skipped around the circle, feeling the dove's little feet in her hair, and so happy that her heart swelled within her.

When they ceased and sat down laughing, to rest on the thick green grass, Rowena found herself beside the boy next whom she had been skipping. He picked up a golden pear and offered it to her.

"Is this heaven?" she asked him as she took it. The dove had flown back to his nest.

"Heaven can be anywhere," he answered, as he picked up a pear for himself and began eating it.

"Not where I came from," replied Rowena decidedly.

"O yes," said the boy, "wherever you are yourself, you can make it."

"That's easy to say," retorted Rowena.

"It's easy to do," said the boy, taking a deep bite of his pear. "You've only to love everybody and look up and to the right."

"If you saw the Polawee river you would know that it isn't very easy to love everybody," said Rowena.

"What's the matter with it?" asked the boy.

"It was a beautiful, clear river when it was named for the Indian Princess, Polawee, and she brought unhappy children to look into it until they stopped crying and were as glad as she was."

"Yes," replied the boy, "but she had her arms around them while they looked. It was her love that helped them."

Rowena turned her head away and thought. When she turned back again she said, "The Polawee is like me. No one loves us. They throw mud and sticks into the river, just as they do at me. They call us both names."

"Then," said the boy, "you and the Polawee should be changed together."

"Yes," said Rowena, "but I am not a fairy like Lily-bud. No one would care what I said, or do anything for my asking."

"O yes, they would," returned the boy so decidedly that it made Rowena wonder if he might possibly be right. "Love is stronger than Lily-bud or any other fairy. Love is always at your side ready to help. If you don't listen to the teasing of the other children, and smile through it and let Love look through your eyes, and you look up and to the right, you will see what will happen. Love will show you how to clean the river, too."

Rowena looked at her companion more closely than she had done before. This was such strange talk for a boy. She saw that he was dressed in white, and for the first time she noticed that wings grew from his shoulders. Then it was that she realized that it was not that all these children were as large as she was, but that she was now as small as they.

"You know a great deal for a boy," she said.

"We are taught a great deal," he answered, "because our king and queen have many errands for us to do when Love directs them."

Rowena was thinking very fast. The pear she was eating was delicious, and it was wonderful to feel the kindness of everybody in this flower-grown, song-laden orchard. The perfume in the air seemed kindness, and the kindness seemed perfume. One moment she longed to stay here forever, but the next the Polawee seemed to be calling her.

She had sometimes seen pigs allowed to walk into the shallow river and stir up the mud with their long snouts. If it were true that Love was always with her, as willing to direct her as to guide the king and queen of fairyland, then surely she should not mind what other children could do to her. She began to long to try her powers. Here in this garden of delight it seemed very easy to look up and Rowena tried not to remember how different were the dust and unkindness of the earth.

She wondered where she could find Lily-bud, and at once the fairy stood before her.

"Are you happy?" she asked.

"Yes, but I must go home," replied Rowena, and Lily-bud saw the new hopefulness in her face.

"Love has given you an errand," she said.

"Yes, yes," replied Rowena, "if I can only have courage!"

"Love is courage," replied Lily-bud.

She waved her wand, and on the edge of the orchard there appeared again a rose-tinted cloud. Rowena could see it gleaming through the branches. She looked about on the happy, winged children who began to rise and fly about among the trees. They accompanied the visitor as far as to the edge of the cloud. Could it be Rowena who was thus pursued with affectionate calls and good wishes and loving looks?

She waved kisses back to them as she and Lily-bud floated away on their rosy couch, down, and down, and down.

The voices grew fainter and fainter until they died away. Rowena was so deep in her thoughts that she did not notice when the cloud itself finally faded into mist and disappeared.

A little red-haired girl in a torn calico dress stood on the bridge over the Polawee. She felt a light kiss on the cheek and looked up and about for Lily-bud; but she saw nothing but the weeping willow tree, dipping its tassels in the dark river. Her eyes rested on the empty tin cans and ashes lying in the edge of the water.

Rowena's first thought was that she should be very late home, and that she would be punished by the aunt with whom she lived.

Her hair was hanging down over her eyes. She had never cared if it did. It shut out some of the things she shrank from seeing.

She hurried off the bridge. She had been away such a long time. How could she explain it? Who would believe her?

One thing Rowena did not know. There is no time in Fairyland. Just as one can in one's sleep go through hours of adventure and awaken to find that it all happened in one minute, so can a delightful visit to Fairyland take place between two whisks of a cow's tail.

The fact is that when Rowena entered the kitchen, expecting a rebuke, her aunt turned from the stove and said:

"It's time to set the table. How untidy you look, child. You've torn your dress again, too."

"Yes, I'll mend it, Aunt," replied Rowena.

Her aunt stared. Such a pleasant answer amazed her, and if she was amazed, Rowena was much more so! She had been gone, as it seemed to her, many hours, and here she was at home in plenty of time to set the table for supper!

"Love must have done that, somehow," she said to herself, and while she worked she thought of the boy in the shining white clothes with whom she had eaten the pear, and she felt again the little pink feet of the dove on her hand,

and heard its gentle coo.

Her poor, torn dress and her snarly hair seemed dreadful to her. She must try to look more like those children in the orchard.

She sat up that night and worked hard to mend her dress and she asked for buttons to put on the places where they were missing. Her aunt put her hand on the child's head. She feared she might be ill, she was so unlike herself, and Rowena, looking up and to the right, saw something very like love looking out of the puzzled woman's eyes.

The next morning when Rowena was ready for school her aunt looked at her again in surprise. Her hair had been brushed until it shone. She looked pink and clean all over from scrubbing with soap and water. Her old dress was whole and properly buttoned down the back.

"My hair gets into my eyes, Aunt," said Rowena. "Have you a ribbon that I could use to hold it back?"

"Yes, I guess so," was the reply and her aunt brought a piece of black ribbon. Rowena tied it around her red locks where the dove's feet had rested.

"I think I'll have to get you a new dress, Rowena, if you are going to be willing to take some care of it."

At this the little girl looked up so pleased that her aunt thought, "She's not such a bad-looking young one, after all," and again Rowena saw something like love looking out of the eyes that usually frowned at her.

"What has got you started on all this?" her aunt asked. Rowena had expected the question and had been wondering how she should answer it. She would have been willing and glad to tell her aunt all about her wonderful visit, but how could she expect to be believed?

"I was standing on the bridge, thinking of the Princess Polawee," she answered. "I was thinking how bad she would feel over the looks of her river. Then I thought that I looked as untidy and muddy as the river myself, and I began to wish I could clean us both up."

Her aunt was so much surprised to hear this that she began to laugh and Rowena heard the pleasure in it.

"You did well to begin with yourself," she replied, "for I'm thinking you will have more trouble with the river. The selectmen of the village don't care how shiftless and careless the people are here. There are laws enough if people only kept them."

Rowena listened to her attentively. "Where are those men?" she asked.

"In the Town Hall, I suppose, if they ever attend to business, but it's everybody for himself in this village."

Now came the dreaded time of every day to Rowena; time to go to school. Usually she prepared an extra scowl and some little clenched fists, ready to fall upon her tormentors as she walked along, but now it seemed a long, long time since yesterday morning and she trudged down the road, saying to herself that Love was beside her, and every few minutes she looked up and to the right.

At last she came in sight of the school-yard and the boys and girls who had arrived early recognized her.

"Hy—Hy—Hyena," they shouted.

Rowena thought of the children in shining white clothes, and the dove's little feet on her hair, and the way its wings had fanned her cheek. She remembered the songs that she had known and sung.

"Hy-ena,

Nobody meaner,"

shouted the boys and girls.

The prickly heat she knew began to course down Rowena's back, but she looked up and to the right and smiled a little as she walked on.

"Hush up," exclaimed one of the children as she drew nearer. "That isn't Rowena."

Rowena heard this and moved on, smiling at the children without a word. Then she entered the school house. As she passed among them they, too, were still, staring at her fair forehead and smiling lips.

Many times during the morning the other children glanced over at Rowena. What had happened to her?

Some of the rougher boys were unwilling to lose the fun of teasing the fiery-tempered little girl, and at recess time they tried it again. Whenever she could not get out of their way she looked up and to the right and was sure to see a lovely cloud or a bird, or a sunbeam—something to remind her of the boy who had told her it was easy to win in a fight like this if one only remembered the rules, and she seemed to the boys so different from their usual victim that they didn't get much satisfaction out of it.

There was a great deal of curiosity about the change in Rowena and one of the older girls at last spoke to her about it.

"What has made you so changed, Rowena?" she asked.

"The Princess Polawee," was the surprising reply.

The big girl told the others and they all laughed as if this were a great joke, but Rowena behaved so quietly and looked up so happily, and her forehead, always before protected by the tangled hair, was so white and smooth, that she seemed altogether like a new being, and stories began to go about the village that Rowena had really talked with the spirit of the beloved Indian maiden, and that the Princess had transformed her.

The effect of these rumors was that there was no more teasing of Rowena. In fact the children stood a little in awe of her, and all the time Rowena was holding in her heart the mission which had made her willing to leave the fairy orchard.

One day, without telling anyone what she intended to do, she made her way to the Town Hall. The men whose duty it was to see that the village was kept in order, and who, Rowena's aunt said, never did it, were sitting around a long table trying to decide whether cows should be allowed to feed in the public park.

Rowena, in her Sunday frock, walked in upon them, and the men took their pipes from their mouths and stared in surprise to see a little girl come in and disturb their conference.

She looked from one to another with eager, bright eyes.

"Are you the selected men?" she asked.

Some of them laughed and some of them frowned. One of the frowning ones said, "Run away, child. What do you mean by coming in here and disturbing us when we are attending to the business of the village?"

"Oh, I'm so glad you do," replied Rowena earnestly. "I heard that you never did attend to it."

At this the laughers laughed harder than ever, and the frowners scowled deeper.

"What does the brat mean? Get right out of here," said one of the latter.

"Hold on, hold on," said one of the laughers. "Let us hear what the child wants. I know who she is. It's little Rowena. Who did you want, child?"

"You," she replied. "All of you. I want the selected men."

"Well, here we are," returned the good natured one. "What's your business?"

"I come for the Princess Polawee, Sir."

Then how all those men stared and again took their pipes out of their mouths. Most of them had heard the story of a child in the village who had been changed by the spirit of the beloved Indian maiden, and even the frowners stopped frowning as they stared at the little girl with the fair forehead and happy, eager eyes.

"Don't talk nonsense," said one of them at last. "The Princess Polawee died before your grandmother was born."

"Yes," replied Rowena, "but her river goes on, and it is sad to see it look so changed since her time. It should be pure and clear as it used to be. Nobody seems to care but the weeping willows, and children can't see themselves in it any more. They think they are ugly and bent and dark, when the river would be so glad to give them back the true picture."

She looked from one to another of the men, hunting for one who seemed to understand.

"That is so," replied one of them, "the river is unsightly. I'm glad I don't live near it. I don't think it's good for a body's health."

"We can't waste time on this," said one of the men impatiently. "Run away, little girl, and dream somewhere else. We have serious business for the village to attend to."

"This is serious business of the village," replied Rowena, and looking up and to the right, her eye happened to catch that of the man who had spoken of health.

"My aunt says there are laws. Aren't there any laws about keeping things clean?"

"Yes, of course there are. But how are you going to make people obey them?"

"I'm not going to," replied Rowena, seriously, "but you will, because unless you promise me, I'm going to find a lawyer."

The selectmen looked at one another.

"The young one is right," said one of them at last; "but why do you care so much, Rowena?"

"Because of the Princess Polawee," she replied. "The children used to call me Hyena until I learned about Love, and the Polawee has been muddied, and bad stuff and cans thrown into it until it looks just the way I used to feel. The Princess knew more about Love than any one who ever lived in this village, and for her sake I am asking you, who were chosen because you were wise men, to help the Polawee to be clean and happy again."

There was another silence, while the selectmen looked at one another and then at Rowena whose face was all alight. Her eyes were lifted as if she saw something beside the ceiling of the ugly room, and she did. She saw the fragrant orchard and the white-clothed children, and heard the joyous singing.

At last one man brought his fist down on the table.

"The youngster is right," he said. "Let the cows go to grass for a while and let us talk about the river. Come here, Rowena." He pulled another chair up to the table. "Come here and join the committee. Now tell us your ideas of how we had better go to work."

Rowena looked very happy and climbed up at once into the chair.

"People have to be punished when they do wrong," she said. "First let everybody know that the Polawee is going to be made so clean that if the Princess came to see herself in it the picture in the water would look as lovely as her own face. Then put up signs that anybody who threw things into the river would have to pay money to you. No tin cans, no ashes, no pigs, no sticks—nothing must go into the Polawee,—then, don't you see," Rowena looked around the table brightly, "don't you see it will wash itself clean, and people will love to go and sit beside it?"

"It is a fact," said one of the selectmen. "The river hasn't been much more than a dump for years. We'll see what can be done about it."

Rowena left the Town Hall after some more talk, and a very happy little girl she was when she ran home and told her aunt what she had done.

Her aunt lifted up her eyes and hands and laughed. "What are we coming to," she said, "when the children have to take a hand! Well, you did wonders, Rowena, to stir up those lazy bones."

The next day in the village paper an article appeared which astonished Rowena's aunt and all the village. One of the selectmen was the editor of the village paper, and fortunately for Rowena it was the one who had looked the most kindly at her and had invited her to sit up at the table. This is what the paper said:

THE PRINCESS POLAWEE IS IN OUR MIDST.

No one who knows the story of the good Indian Princess will be very much surprised to learn that she has not been able to rest in the happy hunting grounds on account of the sad condition of her beloved river.

From its high estate of comforter to the sorrowing, the Polawee has become the poor, ugly dumping ground of all the lazy folk in our village. The Princess, unable to bear any longer the burden put upon her dear stream, has spoken through the lips of one of our own children and pleaded for a restoration of its beauty and charm.

The village fathers, therefore, have decided to comply with the wishes of the Indian Maid and see that the change is brought about. Henceforth the Polawee is to be the object of our loving care until it comes into its own.

Posters will soon appear in convenient places near the river bank, explaining that any and all persons who throw into the water anything more ugly than freshly gathered flowers, will be punished by a fine, the money thus received to go toward further beautifying the Polawee; but we hope that our citizens will so sympathize with the good Princess, and so realize what an ornament the river should be to the village, that we shall receive no money from that source.

(Signed) Your Village Council.

When Rowena's aunt read this she wiped her glasses and gazed at the child and then read the article aloud to her.

Rowena skipped all about the room in her happiness.

"What is all this," asked her aunt, "about the Princess speaking through you?"

"I think that is a joke," replied Rowena. "One of the selected men was funny and nice."

When she went to school the next day the children had all heard what was in the newspaper, and heard that it was Rowena who had spoken for the princess. They whispered among themselves, and when she appeared seemed almost afraid of their changed playmate, but she did not notice this at all. The chief thing any little girl can do to be happy is to forget all about herself, and Rowena's mind was so full of her hopes for the river that she went right up to the other children and said:

"Who will join the Polawee Club?"

"What is that?" asked the others.

"Why," said Rowena, "I think it would be fun to get together and make the bank of the river pretty. The girls can plant flowers and the boys can make benches and put them in the nicest places, and we shall all be helping to make the Polawee become again a good little clear, clean, lovable stream."

The children only stared at first, but Rowena looked so eager and happy, and seemed so changed in the pretty dress which her aunt had told her she could now wear to school, and since even their fathers had listened to her and taken her advice, they began to think that they might do so too.

"All right," said one of the biggest girls, "I'll join the Polawee Club."

"And I, and I, and I," chimed in others. And to make a long story short

Rowena did get them all interested at last, and the fathers and mothers were helped to keep the new rules about ashes and tin cans because their children were loving and helping the river.

Sometimes when the Polawee Club were tired and stopped to rest, they would sit down on the grass and Rowena would tell them stories.

The one they liked best of all was that of a little girl who was sore-hearted and lonely. A fairy named Lily-bud appeared to her one day and took her to the fairies' orchard where the little girl found she could sing, and the other children there were all glad she had come.

She sat on the grass with a boy in shining white clothes and ate delicious pears with him, and he told her of Love, greater than all the fairies. He told her that if in all her troubles she would look up and to the right she would be helped. He said that the Princess Polawee was using Love when she made crying children look into her river; and the little girl listened to it all and was so comforted that she tried what he had told her to do and found that he told the truth.

And while the children planted their flowers and the boys made their benches and Rowena told her stories, the Polawee was washing itself clean.

Love continued to watch over it and at last the weeping willow saw the lovely grace of its branches reflected clearly in the water. The wisps of white cloud and the birds flying over saw themselves in its depths; and whenever a child in that village had a little heartache and wept a little weep, one of the Polawees would lead her to the river and make her laugh at the funny face looking up from the crystal mirror.

But Rowena remembered the words of the boy in shining white:

"Yes, but she had her arms around them while they looked. It was her love that helped them."

CHAPTER VIII.

FAREWELL.

When Lois and Hal went home from their visits to Wenonah they would repeat her stories as well as they could to their father and mother, who liked them very much.

Mr. and Mrs. Robbins gave the Indian maiden many pleasant times in return for her kindness to their children. One day it would be a picnic, another day a sail, and the more they saw of Wenonah the better they liked her.

Mrs. Robbins asked her one day about her Winter home and how she lived; and she could see that the Indian girl, on account of her education, had many trials in the manner of living of her own people. Mrs. Robbins asked her how she would like to go home to Boston with them.

"I am sure," she said, "that those clever fingers of yours must be able to sew as well as weave, and I think you could be very useful in our home. My children are so fond of you they would be delighted I know, if you would come." Wenonah's eyes shone and looked far away, and she smiled.

"That would be happiness," she said, "but I can help my own people and they need me."

There came a day when the Indians took down their tents because the Summer folk were leaving and they could not sell anything more. They went away and took Wenonah with them and Lois and Hal had lumps in their throats when they bade the Indian girl good-bye.

"Another Summer, perhaps," she said to comfort them, and her own eyes grew wet, for the children had been a great joy to her in her loneliness.

She gave them each a sweet-grass basket with a cover as a parting present, and they put them inside the rougher ones they had made themselves. That charming perfume would always make them think of the bright plumage, the shining braids and the flashing eyes of their new friend.

"Please be thinking up stories all Winter, will you, Wenonah?" asked Hal.

She promised; and at Christmas-time the children sent her a book of interesting tales to entertain her through the long, cold Winter evenings as she had entertained them through many a sunny afternoon.

They wrote her, also, of a wonderful Christmas gift they had received, themselves. A baby sister had come to their house and they were trying to decide on a name for her. They wanted to call her Wenonah, they wrote, but their mother said her nose wasn't straight enough!

"But we will tell her all about you," wrote Lois, "and we'll bring her with us next Summer. She's such a little, tiny thing! Hal and I told her about Lily-bud and Rose-Petal and she smiled. We think perhaps she knows them. We can hardly wait until she grows big enough to tell us. Good-bye, Wenonah, Good-bye."